Made for each other?

Usually Caitlin danced by imitating the moves of whomever she was dancing with. With Dom, though, she could feel his body moving in response to hers, as though they were dancing together, a slow dance, instead of a fast one like this, standing feet apart. But then when she turned her back to him, she felt him move close behind her and could sense he was moving in exact imitation of her, their bodies two reeds being swept by the same currents.

THE LAST GREAT SUMMER

CAROL STANLEY

SCHOLASTIC INC.
New York Toronto London Auckland Sydney

No part of this publication may be reproduced in whole or in part, or stored in a retrieval system, or transmitted in any form or by any means, electronic, mechanical, photocopying, recording, or otherwise, without written permission of the publisher. For information regarding permission, write to Scholastic Inc., 730 Broadway, New York, NY 10003.

ISBN 0-590-45705-5

12 11 10 9 8 7 6 5 4 3 2 1   2 3 4 5 6 7/9

Printed in the U.S.A.   01

First Scholastic printing, July 1992

THE LAST GREAT SUMMER

June

Chapter 1

The town of River Bend, Texas, was baking under a white summer sun this Friday afternoon in June. Just outside the town limits, in the wealthy neighborhood of Hickory Hills, Caitlin Carney — fresh from the shower in a T-shirt and shorts, her auburn hair in wet tendrils that touched her shoulders — sat in the humming chill of the house's central air-conditioning. She was sitting up on her bedroom dresser, straight-backed, her face set in the most serious of her many serious expressions as she frantically tried to memorize her valedictory speech. She was going to have to give this for real in just a couple of hours, in front of practically everyone she knew, at the commencement ceremonies at Rio Rojo High School.

". . . and so, as we stand before the open door to life, we can only hope — " she said in what she hoped was her most confident voice.

" — that we don't trip on the welcome mat," finished Patti Costa, who was stretched on Caitlin's water bed, prompting her friend from a typed copy of the speech.

"Patti, you wretch," Caitlin said, laughing in spite of herself. "You're supposed to be coaching me. Come on. Be serious."

Patti made a zipping gesture across her lips, as if to seal them into seriousness.

". . . as we stand before the open door to life, we — "

"We can only hope the doorknob doesn't fall off in our hand," Patti interjected and this time really got to Caitlin, who started laughing so hard her shoulders were shaking.

"You are such a rat. Now, when I get to this part, I'm going to burst out laughing in front of everybody. No. Worse. Everybody *and* their parents."

"Do you good. That's what you need, a few deeply humiliating experiences. There aren't nearly enough of them in your life. You get all A's in school. You're class valedictorian. Your parents are filthy rich, and you've got them wrapped around your little finger so they give you anything you want. See what I mean? You've got no bad parts, no awkward moments, nothing to make you hideously insecure and self-conscious like the rest of us. Remind me to put a banana peel on the steps up to the stage this afternoon, will you?"

"Come on. It's not all roses," Caitlin said. "I don't — if you've noticed — have a hunky boyfriend like Jennifer does. Or a great family, like you do. You might have noticed that living in the Carney

4

household is a lot like living in the middle of a combat zone."

This stopped Patti in her tracks for a moment. It *was* pretty much *The War of the Roses* around the Carney house. When you walked through a room that had both Caitlin's mom and dad in it, your first impulse was to duck. Not that they were ever actually throwing anything. It just felt like they might start any second, and you wanted to be out of there before they did.

"Okay," Patti conceded, "your parents are maniacs, but — "

As if to underline Caitlin's point, there was a burst of shouting from downstairs that ended with Mrs. Carney's voice screaming, "Just shut up, will you!"

Patti could see from the way Caitlin shut her eyes against this that her parents' fighting really got to her.

"Oh, by the way," Patti said, trying to move off an unpleasant subject, "speaking of hunks, my brother just got back."

"Dominick?" Caitlin couldn't imagine why Patti was referring to him as a hunk. It must be sisterly devotion. When he'd gone into the merchant marine two years earlier, Dominick Costa had been a heavyset, hoody type with greasy hair and thick glasses, who hung around with a bunch of guys at Ernie's Shell Station, working on their cars after hours. If Dominick hadn't been Patti's brother, Caitlin wouldn't even have known his name. They lived in the same town, but in different worlds.

"Yeah. He's been all over the world since he left, sailing the seas. Well, you know. I've shown you the postcards. Now he says he's happy to be back on dry land, you know, terra firma. I'm bringing him to the commencement dance tonight. You *will* dance with him, won't you?"

"Sure," Caitlin said. Patti was a good friend. Caitlin would do almost any favor she asked, even dance with her hoody brother. She looked down at her thin, black, Italian designer watch — a graduation gift from her parents. "Yikes!" she said when she saw the time. She jumped off the dresser as though she'd just heard a starting gun go off. "We'd better hustle! We have to be dressed and over at school by two-thirty."

"Ahhh," Patti said, and she stretched across the bed sideways like a cat — her long legs sticking out over one side, her heavy brown hair nearly touching the floor on the other. "I wish I could get more excited about this commencement. Maybe it's just the stupid dress I have to wear to the dance — you know, the one Mom made me."

"How bad *is* it?" Caitlin asked, disappearing into her closet, flipping through a few racks, and coming out with a beautiful sandwashed silk shirt and skirt.

"*My* dress?" Patti said, envying the outfit Caitlin was holding up to herself in front of the mirror. "Basically it looks like what you'd wear if you were going off to join a religious order."

Caitlin nodded. She'd seen other outfits sewn by Mrs. Costa, a woman with a heart of gold and a zero sense of style.

"Just borrow something of mine."

"No. I don't want to hurt my mom's feelings. She worked really hard on it," Patti said. "Besides, the dress isn't the whole reason I don't want today to really happen. The other part is that today is really the last day the rain dancers will all be together — well, you know — officially. Tomorrow really *is* going to be the first day of the rest of our lives."

"Yeah, isn't it exciting?!" Caitlin said, the future catching in her throat a little.

"For *you*. You're going off to Vassar, to some fabulous, sophisticated college life. For me, today is the edge of the abyss. My future is a giant black hole."

"Come on. You've already got a job lined up."

"Yeah. Waitressing at the country club. Stop me from quivering with excitement."

"But that's just temporary," Caitlin said, coming over and holding out a hand to pull Patti off the rippling bed. "Just until you make up your mind what you want to do about college."

"Yeah, right," Patti said, standing up and tugging the legs of her spandex shorts down over her thighs. This was the story she was putting out, that she was still deciding whether or not she wanted to go on to college. The real reason, the one she couldn't tell anyone — especially not Caitlin, who thought "money problems" were when your parents forgot to keep your checking account balance over a thousand dollars — was that *her* parents couldn't afford to send her anywhere, not even to a state school where, even with the lower tuition, there would still be room and board they couldn't pay.

No, Caitlin tried to be sensitive, but there was really no way she could understand what life was like for Patti, in a family where there were so many kids and your dad worked the oil rigs and your mother helped out in a day care center and money was always tight.

"Want a snack before you go?" Caitlin asked Patti, turning as they headed out of the room. "Mom got some caviar for a special graduation treat. Esther made some toast points."

"Thanks anyway," Patti said. "But you know I have that awful allergy to toast points. So tiresome." She waited, but Caitlin didn't get the joke.

Jennifer Novak unplugged the crimper and ran her fingers through her wild, blonde — and now crimped — hair. She knew she was considered the most beautiful girl at Rio Rojo High — people told her this all the time — but she honestly couldn't see this herself. She thought her nose was too thin, her mouth too wide.

And besides, she wanted to be known for more than her looks. When you're pretty, she'd found, your looks get to be a box everyone puts you in. And so she gave herself just the briefest once-over in the mirror, first checking out her dress, which was peach colored, and then her pale blue eyes. "Cornflower blue," her mother called them. They would definitely look better with a little eyeliner and lots of mascara, but she knew any eye makeup she put on would just — especially in this heat —

get smeared the first time she put her eye to the viewfinder of her video camcorder. And she expected to have her eye pressed to that viewfinder most of the afternoon because today history was being made. She and her best friends, the other rain dancers, were graduating. Jennifer and Caitlin and Patti and Leah and Danny, their "token" boy.

Their tight, five-way friendship had started years before, back in fourth grade when their teacher, Mrs. Shute, had cast all of them as Apaches in the annual "Texas History Day" pageant. Leah's mother, who was a librarian, researched tribal rituals and came up with a rain dance they could all do.

The day of the pageant was sunny and hot. The raindance wasn't scheduled until the end of the show. While the earlier acts were going on, the five of them began to practice behind the school. The sky began to cloud over a bit. And then, when they went onstage in their face paint and headdresses and performed their dance for the audience, the clouds began to bunch up and grow darker, and by the time they had finished, they and their audience and the other performers were being drenched by a sudden downpour. At first no one said anything; they just looked around in amazement. Afterward, everyone tried to explain it away. Some of the other kids said it was just coincidence, but the rain dancers looked at each other and knew differently. Ever since that day, the five of them had been as thick as blood brothers — or rather, four blood sisters and one blood brother. Of course they had fights and feuds and didn't always get along. They were all really different personality types — Caitlin so serious, Patti so high-energy, Danny so crazy, Jennifer so ambitious, Leah so sweet and spacey. Sometimes all their different personalities worked together like the inside of a watch. Other times they clashed or got on each other's nerves — like everybody, like every group of friends. What was different about the rain dancers was that no matter what happened — no matter *what* — they stayed friends, stuck together, and knew they always would.

And now, this afternoon, all five of them were graduating, heading off in different directions come fall. This summer would be the last chunk of time they'd share, and Jennifer wanted to catch as much of it as she could on videotape. So that when they were all old and gray, they could look back and show their grandchildren what great friends they had been. Or maybe she would put the tapes into a time capsule. She'd bury them for interplanetary visitors to find a million years into the future and see what being a teenager was like in River Bend, Texas, northern hemisphere, planet Earth, toward the end of the twentieth century.

Her reverie was interrupted by the doorbell chiming from downstairs. She grabbed her videocam, took the steps two at a time and threw open the door. Alan Hansen was standing on the other side of it — tall and gawky in his graduation gown, like a scholastic scarecrow, his pale brown hair combed off his face, his eyes sparkling with anticipation of the big day ahead.

"Love of my life," she said as she pressed the "record" button to catch him as he began blushing. Alan blushed every time she called him the "love of her life," even though they both knew it was true.

Then he took her videocam out of her hand and put his hand on the back of her neck and pulled her toward him. They kissed each other deeply, intensely, as though they hadn't seen each other in years, when in fact it had only been since yesterday. It was always like this with them. Even though they'd been going together for a couple of years, they were still riding a rush of passion. They weren't lovers, and their friends teased them about being too sensible, but they both wanted to wait until they felt better able to handle everything that seemed to come with sex: the change it might make in their relationship, in their feelings toward each other. They both knew waiting was the right thing for them but, still, it was hard doing it, hard fighting back the impulses that came over them whenever they saw each other.

She pulled back to examine him in his graduation gown.

"You look great!" she said, although this was only partly true. He had been one of the cutest boys in River Bend until the terrible car accident he and his family were in a few years ago. After that, he was in and out of the hospital, for rehabilitating his broken leg and for reconstructive surgery on his face, which, except for a thin scar angling down above his left eyebrow, was now pretty much back to normal. But lately he'd been sick, half the time it seemed, with flulike things. He was just getting over the latest bout, and his coloring still had a pale, skim-milk look to it that made Jennifer nervous, made Alan seem too vulnerable. She brushed her worries aside quickly so he wouldn't see them.

"You up for this?" she asked now. "The Big G — graduation?"

"Dum dum da da dum dum," he began singing in a deep voice, an off-key rendition of "Pomp and Circumstance." As he sang, he halt-stepped toward and past her, the way they'd practiced coming down the auditorium aisle in their caps and gowns. When he hit the wall with his forehead, like a short-circuited robot, he turned and said, "I came by on the off-chance your parents wouldn't be making it this afternoon and you might need a ride. My folks are waiting in the car."

"Oh, that's great," Jennifer said. "I was just going to drive over by myself. Dad got called in for some poor guy whose heart went into arrest, and Mom's delivering a baby."

"Yeah, while her own baby walks down the aisle alone," he said. Jennifer was used to Alan's sarcasm about her parents, who he thought neglected their daughter in favor of their fast-track careers as doctors.

"Hey, Alloon!" came a shout from above them, and then suddenly Jennifer's brother Scotty was heading toward them, sliding his way down the bannister, one of the five hundred things he was forbidden to do but did anyway as soon as their parents were out of the house. It was as if Scotty was in some personal lifetime competition to get away with as much as he possibly could.

"I think he's an aspiring criminal," Jennifer said.

Alan nodded as he rumpled Scotty's hair. "I know. I saw some guys in fedoras interviewing him on the middle school playground the other day. They told me they're already on to his potential."

"You *guys!*" Scotty said. "Can I come and watch you graduate?"

"No way," Jennifer said. "If you don't mind, I'd like my commencement exercises to come off without any water balloons thrown from the balcony, which if you remember is what you did when you snuck into my junior prom."

"I've become so much more mature since then," Scotty said, but no one believed this, not even him.

"You're staying here with Mrs. Harris," Jennifer told him. "She's in the kitchen fixing you a nice snack."

"Eye of newt on toad crackers," Scotty said. He didn't like his baby-sitter and was trying to convince Jennifer and their parents that she was a witch.

"I'll report on all the big events for you," Alan said. "And, of course," he added, tapping Jennifer's video camera, "we'll have it all on tape, as we do every other moment of our lives, thanks to your film fiend sister."

There was an impatient blast of honking from the driveway.

"Our chariot awaits," Alan said with a sweeping bow, and Jennifer dashed around the house, looking for her cap and gown.

"Where did I put my mortarboard?" she wailed and then, when Scotty found it on top of the piano in the living room and handed it to her, she turned to Alan and asked, "Why do they call it a mortarboard anyway?"

"I'll tell you when the clock strikes midnight and we're all alone, my darling," he said in a stage actor voice, and as they walked out onto the front porch, he ran down the front steps and tore across the lawn, swooping his open graduation gown around like bat wings.

Chapter 2

"If you keep driving at this snail's pace, we'll miss the whole commencement," Mr. Carney nagged at his wife, who was behind the wheel of the large white Mercedes. "A kid on a bike just passed you. Maybe at this speed, you ought to just drive on the sidewalk. Then only mothers pushing strollers would have to pass you."

"If I let *you* drive, we'd crack up and never get to the commencement," Caitlin's mother said, her jaw set, her eyes glued to the road, her hands in a death grip on the steering wheel. (She was the world's most anxious driver.)

Can't you two stop this for one afternoon — for my graduation!? Caitlin screamed at them inside herself. Even though her parents said they loved her, and were telling her all the time how she was the most important thing in their lives, and bought her practically anything she asked for, they were usually too busy sniping at each other to pay much real attention to her. When people asked Caitlin if she was an only child, she always thought, *No, I'm a lonely child.*

She envied her friend Patti's large, warm family — always laughing or goofing off with each other. Caitlin's parents *never* goofed off. Her father ran Carney Oil. The company was his life. He was down at the office or out at the oil fields before Caitlin woke up in the morning and didn't return home until late at night.

Her mother's life revolved around managing the most perfect household in Texas. She spent her days running a staff of servants ragged. She held luncheons and teas and sit-down dinners for twenty and New Year's Eve buffets for a hundred guests, some of them flown in for the party on the Carney Oil private jet. She knew how flowers should be arranged, invitations replied to; how lobster should be eaten, and how royalty should be addressed. (Not that any royalty had ever turned up at the Carneys' house — she just wanted to be prepared in case any did.)

Caitlin's parents were just as serious and well-organized about Caitlin. It was as if they had her whole future already outlined and tucked away in a file folder. The plan was for her to go off to Vassar in the fall, take a ladylike liberal arts curriculum, and wind up marrying a boy from the Ivy League, not necessarily from a family as rich as theirs, but from one with a higher social status. That is, someone whose money was "older" than theirs. The Carneys' own wealth only went back a generation. Both of Caitlin's grandfathers had struck it rich in oil.

Practically since she was born, her parents had been pushing Caitlin to be the best in games and sports in school. Ever since she could remember, they'd been telling her to stand up straight, to use the proper fork with each course, to look pretty and act sweet. All of which made Caitlin scream silently inside herself where no one could hear. She had no idea what she wanted to do with her life, just so it was *not* exactly what her parents wanted her to do.

Even now, as they pulled up in front of the school, her mother was saying, "Remember your posture."

"And pronounce your words distinctly," her dad said, looking over the seat back at her. "You tend to mutter when you're under pressure."

"Okay," Caitlin said in a voice that sounded very small, even to her. In her dreams she was always small, her parents large, looking down at her, shouting instructions.

"I wonder where everybody is?" Jennifer said to Alan when his parents had gone around back to park after dropping them off in front of the Rio Rojo auditorium. Like the rest of the school, the auditorium had a distinctive southern Texas look — mission style, with adobe walls and orange tile roof. The steps were bordered on both sides by giant cacti. As Jennifer planted her feet wide apart and tried to get an establishing shot of the graduation scene — students and their families greeting each other in an epidemic of smiling — she told Alan, who was waiting patiently at her side, "There are some things about the way Texas looks that I'm really going to miss."

"Southern California isn't going to look all that different," he said. "We'll just have to get used to palm trees instead of cactus."

Jennifer smiled thinking of their future together. She pictured it as a soft green lawn stretching before them all the way to the horizon. Alan could have gone to any college in the country. His SATs were the highest in the school, and the only grade he'd ever gotten lower than an A was in typing. Ms. Crandall said she simply couldn't give an A to someone who typed using only two fingers, no matter how fast he was. (It was this B that caused him to lose the valedictorian spot to Caitlin, who had a perfect all-A record.)

Out of all the schools in the country that would have been happy to have him, Alan picked UCLA because that was where Jennifer had won a special scholarship in film and video. She'd be working with some of the biggest names in the business. It was the chance of a lifetime for her, and Alan knew it. Although he'd been planning to go to Harvard, he immediately switched, and would take his four years of pre-med in California. He planned to be a psychiatrist and said it didn't really matter where he went to school, or wound up practicing. "People will still be crazy to see me."

It was perfect, their going away to college together. Their parents insisted they live in dorms at least for their first year, but they planned to get an apartment together as soon as they could. An apartment meant privacy, a place where they could be lovers — away from prying eyes of parents, free from the possibility of roommates crashing in on them.

"Hey!" Jennifer shouted, coming out from behind her camera when she saw Patti and Caitlin and Leah and Danny making their way through the crowd toward them.

"You guys look so serious and important in those gowns," she said from behind her camera. "I have to capture this for posterity."

"I don't know about the rest of you," Leah Shore said, trying to smash her mortarboard onto her head of spring curls, "but I feel pretty weird. I mean, like, I've been practically my whole life in high school, and now, just when I was getting comfy, it's like they're kicking me out."

"You can't look at it that way," Jennifer said as she motioned to Leah to stand closer to the others so she could get them all in the frame. "I mean, aren't you excited about going off to college, living on your own, meeting all sorts of new people, having all sorts of new experiences?"

"I guess . . ." Leah said, but didn't sound at all convinced by Jennifer's argument. And in spite of how sure she tried to sound in making the argument, Jennifer had to admit that in her heart of hearts she was pretty scared about what the future held and what would be expected of her. High school was safe; college and the wider world and all the decisions and choices she would have to make *were* exciting, but also very scary.

"Are you all going to the dance afterward?" Caitlin asked.

"Sure. I think it'll be fun," Leah said.

"Yeah, right," Danny said, "with our parents there. Give me a break. My dad's going to insist on doing the lambada, I just know it." Like Danny, his father, Mr. Sanchez, was short and stocky and wore glasses — not the type of guy you could easily imagine doing that kind of dance.

"*I'm* going for sure, no matter how weird or corny it's going to be," Patti said, pushing her long mass of dark brown curls back, then picking up her hair with one hand to get it off her neck in the heat. "Tomorrow I start my waitress job at the club. Tonight will be my last time to get treated like a guest there instead of like hired help. Tomorrow I'll be serving all you rich snobs Cokes by the pool."

"Such an insolent girl for a servant," Danny said in a really terrible English accent.

Caitlin picked up on this and fanned herself with an imaginary handkerchief as she strolled into the auditorium, looking like a dotty duchess. "Yes, yes," she said, "it's so hard to get good help these days."

"You creeps. You're going to make this the *Summer from Hell* for me, aren't you?" Patti asked.

"What about poor *me*?" Danny said. "I've got to be your boss! For three months I'm going to have to deal with your attitude."

In addition to their ultrachic restaurant in

town — Playa del Sol — Danny's parents ran the dining room and grill at Hickory Hills Country Club. As a step in grooming Danny to eventually take over the family business, his father was putting him in charge of the grill for the summer. Patti would be working for him, and the situation was a little tense for both of them. The jokes were a way of taking heat off a sensitive issue.

"At least you'll be where something's happening," Leah said. "Thanks to my mother, I'm going to be spending the summer as her assistant at the library. While you're having fun, I'm going to be learning the Dewey decimal system and shushing anyone talking over a whisper."

"We'll come and rescue you," said Jennifer, who was going to be a nurse's aide for the summer on the night shift at River Bend General Hospital, so she'd have at least part of her days free. "We'll take you to lunch at noisy places. The bowling alley."

"The steel refinery," Alan added. "We'll find job sites with jackhammers."

"Hey, you bozos!" Caitlin called out. She'd gone inside the auditorium and now scooted back out to gather up her straggling friends. "I didn't rehearse my stupid speech all week just to have you miss it."

"You're so cute when you're mad," Jennifer teased as she held up the camera and caught Caitlin on video.

"Oh, no," Caitlin moaned. "I knew it. I'm going to wind up on *America's Most Embarrassing Home Videos*."

"Well, if it's embarrassing you're looking for — "

Danny said, throwing open his sombre, dark blue gown to reveal an extremely loud pair of baggy Hawaiian print shorts and a T-shirt that said ELVIS GIVES BIRTH TO EXTRATERRESTRIAL BABY.

"Danny the Desperado," Jennifer said, using his old nickname. "I'm glad to see you're giving this important day the respect it deserves."

"I think there's something pretty comical about them letting *me* graduate. I kept asking Mr. Federly if there wasn't some mistake, a glitch in the computer or something, and he said no, they'd over-ruled the computer and decided to graduate me just to get me out of here." With that, he skated into the auditorium on the roller blades no one had noticed he was also wearing under his long gown.

Danny sat in the hot auditorium with his friends' laughter ringing in his ears. *Keep them laughing,* he thought. *The motto of a clown. But does anyone ever wonder what's really going on inside me?*

The commencement ceremonies were much more impressive than he'd imagined. He'd never taken school too seriously. He had known since forever that what he'd do after graduation was work in his family's restaurant. But today, in the midst of all these solemn speeches and with everyone looking so serious in their navy gowns, with crimsom tassels dangling from their caps, he was suddenly filled with school spirit.

Maybe it was true that you just couldn't really appreciate something until you were about to lose it. And maybe what he was really missing in advance was Leah. In less than three months she'd be heading off to the state university in Austin, while he was going off to a culinary institute in Vermont. And if he didn't do something about it soon, their lives would head in two different directions without her ever knowing how he felt about her.

How he had felt about her secretly for some time now. How he would watch her mouth when she smiled and imagine how her lips — soft, he knew they were soft without having touched them — imagine how they would feel under the pressure of his own. Or he would imagine how her body would feel lying next to his.

He even had the scene all worked out in his head. One night the two of them would be watching a video at his house. No one else would be around. (Even this was a fantasy. There was never a time when nobody was around in a big family like his.) Some romantic movie — maybe *Pretty Woman* — was on, and when Richard Gere leaned in to kiss Julia Roberts, Leah would turn to Danny and look at him in a new way, a way she never had before. She would immediately be overwhelmed by passion for him and fall into his arms.

Of course, she had no idea that any of this went on inside him. To Leah, Danny was just a good friend, an old and trusted one, funny and fun and totally sexless. If anything, after so many years of being part of the otherwise female rain dancers, Danny was pretty sure Leah had come to think of him as one of the girls, an auxiliary girl to confide in and whisper things to when Patti or Caitlin or Jennifer wasn't around. (Once, distractedly at a basketball game, she asked him if she could borrow his lipstick.)

The one thing she definitely did not see was Danny as a potential boyfriend.

He leaned forward in his seat a little, while Caitlin was giving her valedictory speech. Something about a door. He couldn't concentrate on what was happening on the stage when everything he wanted was sitting two rows in front of him. What he saw was that Leah was also leaning forward out of her seat. Without even bothering to follow her sight line, he knew she was trying to catch a glimpse of Greg Wright, who was sitting in the first row. Greg Wright who didn't know Leah Shore existed, the way Leah didn't know Danny existed, except as a funny friend. Was the whole world, Danny wondered miserably, just one long chain of unrequited love?

Chapter 3

The dining room of Hickory Hills Country Club had been decorated (by a committee headed by Caitlin's mother) with about five gardens worth of fresh flowers — along the entryway, on the tables, at the back of the bandstand, where there hung a sign made of carnations — a background of blue tinted blossoms with red flowers spelling RIO ROJO GRADS!

The club, like the community of Hickory Hills it was situated in, had been built by oil. That is, it had been opened years and years ago as a playground for the new oil millionaires around River Bend and their families. The golf course was an oasis of green in a landscape of scrub land, short hills, and red clay river banks. There were outdoor tennis courts as well as indoor, air-conditioned ones for the hot, hot days of Texas summers. The pool was Olympic-size, and there was also a small beach rimming a blue lake. The dining room was one of the most elegant restaurants in the area, and the grill was the gathering place for the cool (and rich) kids from Rio Rojo High.

The club had been a part of Caitlin's life for so long that she took its privileges for granted. Tonight, she didn't even notice the gold-edged china, the sterling, and the crystal that decked the white-linen draped tables. Of course, she was too angry to notice much of anything really, arriving long after everyone else because of an argument her parents had gotten into over where they should park.

Why don't they just get a divorce? Caitlin thought as she led them across the dance floor, searching for her friends. The rain dancers and their families had arranged to sit at the same long table for the graduation dinner (Texas steaks and French cuisine) and the dance that would follow (music provided by a rock band from Dallas — Last Stand). Caitlin's mood shifted when she saw all of them together tonight, these people who were so important in her life, a kind of large, extended family that in many ways had made up for the shortcomings of her own, nuclear (*really* nuclear!) family.

Her warm thought — how familiar all these faces were to her — was suddenly interrupted by the distinctly *un*familiar face of the guy sitting next to Patti. And what a face! Dark and brooding, sort of a combination of Elvis and James Dean and Jason Priestley. And his hair — jet black and curly and long in back. *Wow!* was all she could think. Was this some secret boyfriend Patti had been hiding? Caitlin had to admit, if she had a boyfriend who looked like this, she might keep him under wraps, too.

As she and her mother and dad took their seats

at the end of the table, she flashed Patti a question mark look, as if to say, "Who is this hunk?" But all Patti did was nod and smile, as though Caitlin was in on the secret. She had to wait all the way through the appetizer and salad courses (trying not to look directly at him; if he saw her expression, he'd probably think she was a complete goon) until she got a clue to the mysterious stranger's identity. It came up when the conversation between a few of the fathers had turned to the subject of oil (the one subject that bored Caitlin more than any other in the world), and Patti beamed at Mr. Terrific and said, "Well, Dom was on an oil freighter for a while, weren't you?"

Dom?! Dominick?! Caitlin couldn't match up her ears and eyes. What she was hearing bore no correspondence to what she was seeing. Dominick Costa was a goony hood. This guy was hunkomatic. It couldn't be the same person.

But it was.

"Looks like being out at sea did you a world of good, fella," Danny's father said, but it had to be what everyone else at the table was thinking. The change was astonishing.

"It was okay," Dominick (the *new*, *improved* Dominick, Caitlin couldn't help thinking) mumbled. Being a sailor clearly wasn't his number one favorite subject. (What *are* his favorite subjects? Caitlin wondered.)

The main course, dessert, and coffee passed by her in a blur. All she could think of was Dom sitting five people down and across the table from her, looking so incredibly cool in his dress clothes — a slouchy black sport jacket, white shirt buttoned at the neck.

When the meal was over (finally!) and the band began playing, Patti came scooting around the table to Caitlin to say, "Remember you promised you'd dance with my brother. You can't go back on a promise, you know."

Caitlin tried to keep from laughing as she looked her friend straight in the eye and said, "I wouldn't think of it, Patti. A promise is a promise."

She let Patti bring her around to where Dom was. As they approached, he stood up politely.

"Dom, you remember Caitlin?"

"How could I forget?" he said in a soft way that was so full of implications Caitlin felt the words pour through her like honey.

"Uh," Caitlin heard herself stumble, "would you like to dance or something?"

"I think dance," he said, again with a sly half-smile on his face as he looked straight into her eyes. "I'm not very good at 'something.' "

Usually Caitlin danced by imitating the moves of whomever she was dancing with. With Dom, though, she could feel his body moving in response to hers, as though they were dancing together, a slow dance, instead of a fast one like this, standing feet apart. But then when she turned her back to him, she felt him move close behind her and could sense he was moving in exact imitation of her, their bodies two reeds being swept by the same currents.

When they'd danced three fast numbers in a row,

the band finally (she thought they never would) started playing a slow song. She waited to see if Dom would ask her to stay out on the floor. So far he hadn't said one word to her. The loud music made talking impossible. But now surely he'd have to say something.

He didn't, though. All he did was take Caitlin's hand and pull it up onto his shoulder, then put his arm around her waist and draw her in toward him, moving into the music. It was so sexy she thought she'd faint.

She didn't, of course. She only swayed a little in his arms. She had never felt this kind of magnetism toward any guy. Of course, the few she'd gone out with — for a month here, a few weeks there — wouldn't exactly be the stars of anyone's romantic fantasies.

Guys like Brice Fraser. His father, Brice Fraser Sr., was the richest man in town; owned half the land in the area, many of the buildings downtown, and a few oil wells to boot. Even Hickory Hills wasn't posh enough for the Frasers, who lived outside town in a fenced-in compound with a pool and tennis courts — even a landing strip for the family's private plane.

Beyond his family's status and money, though, Brice didn't have much to offer. He was not particularly good-looking (although because of his buzz cut hair, you *did* notice him), nor was he particularly bright or witty; he wasn't a sports star or a sharp dresser. Still, because he knew that everyone knew who he was, he acted aloof and snobby around school. And from the time she started dating him, Caitlin found there was something icky about him, an odd, smirking sort of negativity. He had something critical to say about everyone — teachers, other kids at school — as though he saw himself as a cut above the rest of the human population.

After a couple of dates listening to his low opinions of everyone else, and his inflated notions about himself, Caitlin made excuses the next few times he called, until he finally stopped calling. Even now, though, when they ran into each other at school, like they did in the auditorium earlier tonight, he acted overly familiar, as though they'd had some big secret affair somewhere in the past. Basically, Caitlin would have to say Brice Fraser gave her a vague set of the creeps. Nothing she could put her finger on, but still . . .

Guys like Brice — rich but weird, or big sports stars who couldn't talk about anything but football or hockey, or guys who couldn't talk about anything but their cars — these were the sort of discouraging dates that made up Caitlin's entire romantic résumé. Until tonight. Until the moment she'd seen Dom and felt the electricity crackle in the air between them. From that moment on, everyone and everything else around her receded into a kind of background. Since she'd come out onto the dance floor with him, everything besides the two of them and the music had simply disappeared into irrelevance. And yet, barely a word had passed between them.

Now, though, dancing slow and close enough that

she could breathe in his mix of sweat and after-shave, now that his mouth brushed her ear, he spoke to her for the first time since his saying "Okay" to her invitation to dance.

"I always liked you best of all my sister's friends," he said now.

She pulled back and looked at him with surprise. She wasn't flirting at all when she said, "I can't believe you even noticed me."

"I notice a lot," he said cryptically.

The slow number had ended, and Caitlin didn't want to break the mood between them. She could tell he didn't want to either.

"Maybe we could go out on the terrace," she said. "Get away from the noise?" Silently she added, *And away from the curious eyes of your family and mine, and all my friends*.

He nodded, as if reading her thoughts as well as her words. He kept a hand lightly on her shoulder as he followed her through the open French doors to the terrace overlooking the golf course, its green supersaturated by a molten, late-setting summer sun.

Jennifer, sitting with Alan at their table, looked around the dining room, seeing all her classmates, now high school graduates, gathered together in one of her favorite places. She loved the club. She and Scotty had spent their summers there for as long as she could remember. Playing tennis, hitting balls at the driving range, but mostly hanging out at the pool with their friends. Almost everyone she knew belonged, except Patti, who always just came along as a guest with one or another of them, so it was almost as though she were a member, too.

The club was also where Jennifer met Alan two summers before. Although they'd passed each other in the halls at school a hundred times, she didn't really know him until they both took the same tennis intensive at Hickory Hills and wound up as doubles partners. After their first match, they went over to the club grill for a Coke; then when they were finished, ordered another, and then he walked her home; but they still couldn't stop talking and didn't want to leave each other, so she walked *him* to *his* house, both of them laughing most of the way. And it had pretty much been like that ever since.

One of the first things he told her about himself was the accident. This — a bad skid into a concrete abutment — happened on an icy winter night seven years earlier, just before New Year's. Everyone in Alan's family had gotten off with cuts and scrapes, except him. He'd been thrown out onto the pavement of the highway and was in critical condition for several days before they even knew if he'd pull through or not. They had to put a pin in one of his legs at the hip, and he still walked with a slight limp, which he refused to let discourage him from playing sports. It was months, and two operations, before his face was back to roughly how he'd looked before.

Jennifer thought this was enough suffering for one person for a lifetime, but now, this year, he'd started getting sick all the time, spending weeks and weeks out of school with one virus, then another. Somehow he'd managed to keep his grades up through all this so he could graduate with Jennifer.

And so tonight she just wanted to forget everything bad that had happened. Tonight she just wanted them to be like any other regular, normal teen couple — having fun, making plans.

They were having coffee and watching everyone out on the dance floor. Specifically, Jennifer was watching Caitlin, who'd nabbed Dom Costa for this "Ladies' Choice" number.

"I wonder if something's brewing with Caitlin and Patti's brother. The way they're dancing is so hot they're practically in meltdown. Oh, Alan, come on. Even though we're an old, practically married couple, we can still get out there and get sexy like these new flames."

"Uh, well, I don't know if I'm quite up to dancing at the moment," he said to her. She could see it was true. He seemed even paler than usual, and a light sweat covered his forehead.

"Oh, Alan," Jennifer said. "Do you want to go home?"

"Maybe soon." She felt dragged — she'd been hoping to get him out on the dance floor — and then immediately felt selfish and creepy for feeling dragged when he was the one who was sick.

"Maybe we could just go outside for a while," he said, seeing her disappointment. "I feel like I need air and can't get enough of it in here with all these people."

"Hey, sure," Jennifer said.

"There's something I need to talk with you about," Alan said when they were sitting together at the edge of the pool. They'd taken off their shoes and were dangling their feet in the cool water.

"So, shoot," Jennifer said, trying to sound casual, even though she was dreading whatever was coming. Alan's tone was so serious. It wasn't like him.

"You know all these flu things I've been getting?"

"Yeah?"

"Well, the doctors are worried. It might be more than the flu."

"Like what? Super Flu?" She could usually change his mood with a joke or two, but this time he wasn't coming around.

"They think I ought to get tested."

"Tested for what?"

"Maybe nothing. It could be lots of things."

"Like?"

"It may even *be* nothing, but they think I ought to get tested for the HIV virus."

"You mean tested for AIDS?! But you're not a drug user. You're not gay. You haven't slept with anyone of *any* sex. You haven't even slept with me."

"I still need to get tested. I got a *lot* of new blood with all those transfusions I had after the accident. Now I've got this wimpy immune system that's not fighting off these infections I keep getting. They think there might be a connection."

34

"But *you* don't think . . . ?" Jennifer said and looked up at him, hoping to make him say what she wanted to hear — that he was going to get better, that he was going to be fine. But instead, he shook his head.

"I don't know."

"It's just impossible," Jennifer said. "You are simply not the kind of person who'd get AIDS. You don't have it and that's *that*."

Jennifer put her arms around him and held him. She closed her eyes and pretended it was last summer and she was here at the pool with Alan, a healthy Alan, with lots of future ahead of them. Last summer, when they had all the time in the world together.

Caitlin could feel the light pressure of Dom's fingers lacing themselves through her own as they stood next to each other watching the sunset. Neither of them seemed to feel the need to make idle conversation; it was as though they'd already wordlessly passed over that phase. And then he was turning toward her and reaching up to touch the side of her face with his fingertips as he said, "I've got to work tomorrow, but what about Sunday?"

She nodded. "Sounds good," she said, hoping she seemed casual, as opposed to how she felt, which was as though a volcano was erupting inside her.

"Meet me down at the river? About noon? We can swim," he said. "I'd come by for you, but I'm not too good with parents."

"It's okay. I'll meet you at High Banks. I'll pack some sandwiches."

He just smiled at this, as though High Banks was the most wonderful place in the world, and sandwiches were the nicest present on earth. Caitlin felt herself going all jellylike around the knees.

"Hey, Cait!" someone shouted, barging into this most perfect moment. Caitlin looked over. It was Leah, looking wonderfully goofy in her dress and mortarboard, which was now sitting atop her springy curls at a jaunty angle. She was driving a golf cart, ready to go. "Come on," she said and motioned to Caitlin. "Hop in. Rain dancers' farewell out on the ninth green." She nodded to include Dom. "Friends are welcome, too."

But Dom shook his head.

"I'd better get home. Got something I need to do."

Caitlin knew at once it was a lie and suspected he just didn't want to break the magic by rushing off to a rowdy party situation. She had no choice, though. The rain dancers had planned this private mini-commencement a couple of weeks back. She couldn't duck out now and didn't really want to. In a way she was glad Dom didn't want to come. She needed to hold him in a private place just now, keep him all to herself until she understood better the tumble of feelings he created in her.

"Gotta go," she said and smiled at him as she ran down the steps and hopped into the golf cart next to Leah. She turned and gave him a quick wave as Leah stepped on the accelerator and they lurched off, burning up the batteries down the fairway.

"New friend?" Leah asked when they'd driven a ways across the course. She put as much innuendo in the question as she could.

"Maybe," was all Caitlin said. Everything that had happened (which was practically nothing really, when she looked back on the past hour) seemed so new and so fragile that she feared talking about it with someone else might make it all vanish in a puff of smoke.

The others rode over together in another car — Patti at the wheel with Jennifer beside her, Danny and Alan clinging to the back for dear life as they stood perilously in the bag racks. When they got to the ninth hole, Danny jumped off and pulled from the duffle slung over his shoulder a bottle of champagne and a stack of plastic glasses.

"Where'd you get this?" Alan asked, taking the bottle and reading aloud from its label. "Mumms."

"Nothing but the best for my friends," Danny said. "And when my dad notices this is missing from the club wine cellar, I'll say there was an unfortunate accident when I was cleaning up down there."

"And he'll believe that?" Jennifer said.

"No. He'll probably ground me for a month. But what are great moments if you don't have to pay for them?" He pressed against the cork with both thumbs and, just as Caitlin and Leah drove up, a huge pop rang through the clear air of dusk. Everyone rushed to get their glasses under the lava of flowing bubbles.

"A one-cork salute!" Danny said, laughing.

"Someone should propose a toast," Alan said, but before anyone could, they all heard the buzz of yet another cart coming over the rise.

"Uh-oh," Leah said. "Security."

"Worse," Caitlin said as the cart came into view. "It's Brice Fraser."

"What's he doing in a staff cart?" Patti said.

"You apparently haven't heard the bad news," Danny said. "He's caddying here this summer. His father thinks a job will be character-building for him. I'd say Brice is enough of a character already."

By now Brice had driven to the edge of the green. He stopped the cart but didn't get out.

"Just checking to make sure everyone's having a good time," he said.

No one could quite think of a response to this, and so they all just said hi to him or nodded a greeting.

"We'll just put that bottle on your tab then, Sanchez," he said, needling Danny, then drove off laughing a loud, self-conscious laugh.

"What's with that guy anyway?" Patti asked.

Caitlin shook her head. "I'm not sure. I think he's our own personal weirdo. I spent two dates trying to figure out what his problem was, but I gave up. I think he's harmless, though."

"I wonder about that," Danny said.

"Forget the creep," Jennifer said. "He's not going to spoil our good time. We're here to propose an important toast. Now if only someone can think of what it is."

"I've got it," Leah said. "To the last great summer!"

They all raised their glasses to this, though each of them put a different emphasis on Leah's words.

For Patti, the important word was "summer," since after this one, there was only the great void for her.

For Caitlin, as thoughts of Dom drifted back into her head, the key word was "great."

For Jennifer, as she looked over at Alan, the word she hoped wasn't significant was "last."

Chapter 4

"Will you spread some of this on my back?" Leah asked, handing a tube of sunscreen lotion to Caitlin. It was Saturday afternoon at the country club, the day after graduation. Patti and Danny were already working in the grill, but Leah's and Jenny's jobs didn't start until Monday, so they were just hanging with Caitlin, who wasn't planning to work at all this summer.

Caitlin looked at the label on the tube Leah had just handed her. "SPF-40? What's in here — a lead shield?"

"My mother says you can't be too careful," Leah said defensively.

"Your mother wouldn't let you cross the street alone until you were in junior high," Caitlin pointed out.

"No, she's right," Jennifer said. "My parents say so, too. Tanning's out now, along with cigarettes and red meat. We're living in the healthy age." As she was talking, she became distracted. "Leah, what's different about your hair?"

"Uh, well, I put a rinse on it for graduation. It was supposed to bring out my blonde highlights." Leah's round face puckered into a frown.

"I think it backfired," Jennifer teased, lifting her sunglasses to peer more closely. "It looks more like it brought out your *green* highlights."

Leah looked up sharply, alarmed.

"Just kidding," Jennifer said and ducked away from Leah's beach towel, which was wadded up in a ball and headed her way.

"Uh oh," Leah's voice shifted down to a whisper. "There he is." The way she said it, HE was in capitals. Caitlin and Jennifer looked up and saw that the object of this awe was Greg Wright, who was one of the club's lifeguards this summer. He had a perfect "swimmer's build," broad shoulders and a flat, muscled chest, tapering down to a washboard stomach and no hips. Even though it was still only June, Greg already had a deep brown tan and light brown hair that was going blond at the tips from the sun.

"Oh, no," Jennifer moaned. "Greg 'You May Kiss the Ground I Walk On' Wright. I can't believe you're stuck on the most conceited guy in our class, Leah."

"It's lifeguard-itis," Caitlin explained. "Everyone gets a case of it sooner or later. Remember the summer I was obsessed with Grif Patterson?"

"How could we forget?" Jennifer said. "By August we were plotting to drown you in the wading pool just so we wouldn't have to listen to one more whimper when he came on shift and climbed up into his chair."

"This is different," Leah protested. "As you very well know, I was obsessed with Greg way *before* he got the lifeguard job, when he was just an incredibly cute guy on a motorcycle."

"I can see this is an attraction based on deeper values — Greg's intellect, his humanitarian spirit," Caitlin teased.

"But he *is* smart," Leah said. "He was in English class with me and Danny. He gave brilliant book reports."

"So . . ." Jennifer said, trying to tread carefully around Leah's feelings, but also trying to determine how reality-based this attraction was ". . . how well did you and Greg get to know each other in English class?"

"Well, once, after he'd been out a day, he asked me if Mrs. Dunn had given any homework."

Jennifer and Caitlin both looked at Leah, waiting for more. When it was clear there wasn't more, Caitlin asked, to make sure, "That's it? That's the sum total of your conversation with him?"

"Well, there was the part where I told him no, she hadn't given any take-home assignment."

Jennifer and Caitlin flopped back on their chaises, groaning and laughing at the same time.

"Come on, you guys!" Leah pleaded. "He might look over."

"He won't," Caitlin said. "Trust me. Greg Wright is too stuck on himself to take the time to look at anyone else. Notice his reflector shades? They're really little mirrors."

"Hey, speaking of juicy romances," Jennifer said,

"you haven't told us a thing, Cait, about . . ." She nodded toward the golf course where Dom was riding back and forth on the huge power mower, wearing only jeans, his back and shoulders and chest dark and glistening with sweat, a white towel hanging around his neck, a red bandanna tied as a sweatband around his head. She could see out of the corner of her eye that he was casting occasional looks her way. She was trying not to look too obviously back at him. Every time she did, she felt weird feelings rushing through her, and she wasn't sure they didn't show on her face. For the time being at least, she wanted to keep her fascination with him to herself. She didn't want him to see, and she wasn't even quite ready for her best friends to see either.

"Well, whatever are you talking about?" Caitlin said, her Texas drawl thickening to cover her nervousness. "I only had a couple of dances with the guy. As a favor to Patti."

"Yeah, right," said Leah. "That's why you two were standing out on the terrace looking like the cover of one of those windswept romance novels."

Caitlin put her sunglasses back on so the other two wouldn't be able to read anything in her eyes. She wasn't ready to talk with anyone about Dom just yet. She'd barely had a chance to begin sorting out her own feelings about him.

He wasn't at all the type she would have predicted she'd fall for. For one thing, he didn't seem particularly brainy, and the guy she'd always had in her fantasies was super-smart. For another, Dom wasn't rich and didn't look like he ever would be. He hadn't gone to college and, even now that he was back home, the job he'd taken — and it was a for-real job as opposed to a summer job —was greenskeeper here at the club. Caitlin could just see her parents' reaction when she told them she was going out with a guy who mowed lawns for a living. They'd go through the roof.

Of course, she didn't have to tell them. Not right away anyway. She'd just say she was going on a picnic with her girlfriends tomorrow. She realized as she thought this, that she'd never actually planned lying to her parents before. She'd never had to. She'd never done anything the slightest bit off from their plans for her. In one way, this made her feel guilty and nervous, but in another way she felt exhilarated, like a parakeet whose cage door has been left open.

"I'm going to ask Greg if he can watch my back flip," Leah said to no one in particular as she got up from her chaise and tugged her bathing suit down around her slightly chubby thighs. "I've been working on it a little, and I know he's a great diver."

Caitlin and Jennifer watched her go over to the lifeguard chair, but it was too far away for them to hear what she was saying.

"You guys look so lazy I can hardly stand it."

They both looked up to see Patti, who'd come out of the grill's poolside entrance.

"My boss — Danny Sanchez to you — says I'm

supposed to ask everyone around the pool if they'd like anything to drink."

"Our waitress has arrived," Jennifer said in a tone she hoped came across as kidding around. It was a little weird being served by a good friend, and she wanted to smooth over the weirdness since it was going to be happening all summer.

"I'll have a Coke," Caitlin said a little distractedly, still absorbed in watching Leah.

"Me, too," Jennifer said and then, seeing that Patti didn't know what was going on, added, "We're watching Leah make a fool of herself over Greg Wright."

"I thought he went with Shannon Christopher."

"Leah is not operating from planet Earth on this. She's orbiting in her shuttle," Jennifer said.

"I think I'm going to avoid romance altogether," Patti said. "I'm going to be a hip, cool old maid."

But the other two were by now totally absorbed in what had or hadn't happened between Greg and Leah, who was now walking back toward them. They hadn't heard a thing Patti had said.

"Listen," Patti said, "I gotta go now. I'll bring your sodas out in a minute."

"Right," Jennifer said distractedly as Patti left, her mind on Leah, who she could already tell — just by her glum expression — had been rebuffed by Greg.

Leah didn't say anything; she just sat back down on her chaise and put her Walkman earphones in and her sunglasses on.

Jennifer pulled the earphones out. "Come on. We're your two best friends. You've got to tell us. We promise not to say we told you so or to laugh, don't we, Cait?"

"Wild horses couldn't drag even a giggle out of me," Caitlin said.

Leah looked down and mumbled, "He said it was against the rules to give coaching while on duty."

"Well, that seems reasonable," Caitlin said, trying to make Leah feel like less of a dope than she already did.

"Yeah," Jennifer added to be supportive. "I've heard that's a very strictly enforced rule, too." This was a total lie. She'd never heard of any such rule. And even if there was one, there was nobody in the pool at the moment and so he wouldn't exactly risk missing a drowning by watching Leah's dive. In fact, as lifeguard, he was practically *required* to watch her when she dove. It didn't look good for this romance taking off.

"Yeah?" Leah said, a note of hope in her voice. "Well, I don't want to get him in trouble. And I do think he looked really sorry he wouldn't be able to do it. There was something in the way he said it, something really sexy, if you know what I mean."

The other two rolled onto their stomachs so they wouldn't have to continue the conversation.

In the kitchen, Patti had five separate drink orders and, now that she looked down at the slips, she realized she hadn't marked the chaises they came from and so had no idea which drinks and sandwiches belonged to whom.

"Oh, Danny!" she said, rolling her eyes, "I'm going to flunk out of this job, aren't I?"

"No way," he said and gave her a hug of support. "I cut my employees a lot of slack on their first days."

Just then, the back door of the club kitchen opened, and Brice came lumbering through, mopping the sweat off his forehead and neck with a towel.

"I've got a thirsty foursome out there — Doc McPherson and his cronies. Can you give me three iced teas and a lemonade?"

"Sure thing," Danny said, setting out four paper cups and filling them with ice scooped from the freezer.

"What a bunch of geezers," Brice said, nodding his head out toward the patio where Doc and his friends were sitting. "You practically have to help them in and out of their carts."

"Well, isn't Doc like eighty or something?" Patti said. Doc was the vet who had saved her dog Trixie's life a few years before, after she'd got into some poison in a neighbor's garden shed. As far as Patti was concerned, Doc was a great person.

"Yeah," Brice said. "All four of them have got one foot in the grave and the other on a banana peel. I'm being incredibly charming to them, though. It's easy, really. I just pretend I think they're great and I don't let them see I'm puking behind their backs."

"Brice," Danny said, "here are your drinks."

Brice didn't take the hint to leave. Instead, he leaned against the counter and said, "They can wait a little longer. It'll do them good to be parched for a while. With all their money, they never have to wait for anything. I'll be building their character. Just like my dad's building mine with this job."

Danny looked over Brice's shoulder and said in a loud voice, "Doctor McPherson!"

Brice jumped about two feet, and only then saw Patti and Danny bursting into laughter.

"Gotcha!" Danny said, to show it was only a joke.

"Yeah," Brice said with his mouth in a sneer and a snarl in his voice, "well, no one *gets* Brice Fraser. You hear me you little greaseball?"

Danny stayed calm, but Patti knew he'd been stung. Racial slurs were just not cool around Rio Rojo, so Danny wasn't used to them. Patti could see his lower lip tremble just a little as he pulled rank on Brice and said in a low voice, "Get out of my kitchen. And keep out of my way."

The two of them stood for what seemed to Patti like several minutes, but was probably only seconds, until Brice finally turned and left. It was clear that a deep, fierce, mutual hatred had begun.

Chapter 5

"A picnic. How nice," said Mrs. Carney as she came into the kitchen where Caitlin and Esther, their cook, were wrapping sandwiches neatly in foil, placing them in an open wicker basket on the counter.

Her mother usually had Esther bring her breakfast up to her on the terrace off the master bedroom. She didn't usually come downstairs until early afternoon; in fact, Caitlin had counted on this. But now, with her mother standing right there, poking through the contents of the basket — brownies and apples and a thermos of lemonade along with the sandwiches — Caitlin was going to have to come up with a bunch of lies she had hoped to avoid.

"Who's going?" her mother asked, requiring the first lie.

"Oh, you know," Caitlin said, waving a hand through the air to show it was almost irrelevant who was coming. "Leah. Patti. Jen."

"I thought Patti was already waitressing over at the club."

"Yeah, well, it's a weird schedule. Sunday's her

day off this week, even though she just started."

Her mother nodded.

"Going to High Banks?" she asked, noticing the swim suit and towel rolled together, sitting next to the picnic basket.

Caitlin nodded. At least this part was the truth. High Banks was a large clearing in the woods down by the Rio Rojo, the red river. The red came from the color of the clay along its banks. The deep blue of the water cutting through the rust color of the ground and the green of the scrub pines made High Banks a beautiful spot for swimming and picnicking.

Caitlin had done very little lying in her life and now found she was terrible at it. It was stupid to have told her mother that Patti was coming along. Now if she went over to the club and Patti came up to take her grill order, Caitlin was sunk. Also, High Banks was a popular spot. Anyone could be there this afternoon, see her with Dom, and mention this to her mother at the beauty salon or the mall or at a bridge game. Argh. She was just going to have to hope her luck held today and work at being a better liar in the future. Because lying was really her only option. Telling the truth was impossible. The first time she told her parents she was going out with a guy with no money and no college degree and a job mowing lawns and a too-hot-to-handle look about him would be the last of Dom Costa in her life.

"Well, have a nice time," her mother said distractedly. She was never very focused before her first cup of coffee. Maybe she wouldn't even remember this whole conversation. Caitlin could only hope.

She took the basket and grabbed her suit, towel, and car keys and sailed out the kitchen door with a wave to her mother and a hug and "Thanks" to Esther. She really didn't have to leave for another half hour, but she didn't want to hang around for more "Twenty Questions."

The heat was incredible, shimmering in waves up off the fields beyond the lawn. Caitlin ran past the stables where the Carneys kept their horses — Nightmare, Black Star, and Caitlin's mare, Honky Tonk. She pushed the button at the side of the middle garage door and waited for the door to open. Inside the garage, she set the picnic basket gently in the boot of her new, blue Miata convertible, another graduation present from her parents.

She felt her heart racing as she pulled the car out, turned it around, and headed down the long, tree-lined drive to the county road, and then onto the highway away from town, toward the river. She loved driving this little car, feeling the wind rushing through her thick, dark red hair, the sun hitting her face. She loved being eighteen and on the brink of life's adventures. Plus this fall, she would be leaving home. Although she loved her parents, she was exhausted with their running battles, tired of trying not to get in the middle or be forced to take sides. She had overheard them one night talking about how they were only staying together on account of her. Couldn't they see how their constant fighting was tearing her up? Couldn't they *stop* on account of her?

She could remember a time when they had been close, even loving, with each other. When she was little and her parents' marriage was still fresh and full of hope. Sometimes Caitlin longed for that time. She'd trade her horse and car and checking account, their beautiful house, all the expensive vacations — everything — to have her family back together the way they had been in those days. This longing for a past that was never going to happen again was a sadness she carried always as a part of her, a secret part underneath the bright, no-nonsense super-achiever everyone thought was the sum total of Caitlin Carney. They were wrong.

She took the turnoff for High Banks and slowed down after looking at the dashboard clock. She was fifteen minutes early, decidedly uncool. Everyone said you were supposed to keep guys waiting a little, not to look overeager. She pulled over and checked herself out in the rearview mirror. Sometimes — particularly in moments connected with guys — she wished she was drop-dead gorgeous, like Jennifer. Or dark and sultry like Patti. Instead of "old-fashioned" or "squeaky-clean" or "rosy-cheeked" — all the adjectives people had used to describe her since she was little. If life were a movie, she'd always be cast as the good girl, the girl next door.

Until now. There was something about Dom Costa that made her feel different. She liked this feeling. She reached in the glove compartment, pulled out her cologne bottle, and sprayed around her neck.

When she pulled into the small parking area, still early, she found that Dom was already there, sitting on the hood of an ancient black pickup truck in faded jeans and a white T-shirt with the sleeves rolled up over his tanned, muscled arms. He was holding a rolled-up towel, with his swimsuit inside, she guessed. He was wearing aviator sunglasses, so it was hard for her to read his eyes. But she knew he was pleased to see her by the slow smile spreading across his face as she pulled up beside him and turned off the Miata's ignition.

"I love girls in convertibles," he said. "Especially redheaded girls in blue convertibles."

This wasn't exactly the most brilliant line Caitlin had ever heard. Why then, did it produce this huge wave of feeling all through her, as if she were hearing him with her whole body, not just with her ears?

"That's funny," she heard herself say, "because I really like guys with black hair and black pickup trucks."

Once again, it was like they were two movie stars in the same sexy scene. She could almost hear the background music. Her usual guy shyness melted away with him. With him, she felt she could say anything and it would automatically be the right thing.

"You're early," he teased her. "Didn't anyone tell you you're supposed to keep me waiting?"

Caitlin felt herself flushing. "I could leave and come back later," she said, "if that'd torture you a little."

He slid down off the pickup's hood and into the passenger seat of her car, and said in a low voice, "I'm already tortured enough waiting through all of yesterday."

Caitlin nodded. She'd felt the same way.

"Let's go up river a little ways," he said. "It's too crowded here. I know a better place."

He gave directions while Caitlin drove. Having lived in River Bend her whole life and ridden horseback over most of the neighboring area, she was surprised when, after following Dom's directions, they came out of the woods at a place she'd never seen before — a clearing on the water with a row of rotted canoe slips and an old lodge house with a screened porch.

Clearly it was deserted and had been for some time. The canoes that were once tied up here were long gone. The lodge itself had been dunned by wind and rain and the relentless Texas sun through enough seasons to wear its many coats of paint away in patches revealing former lives of green and tan and brown and — improbably — a few stacks of faded pink.

"It's the old Red River canoe camp," Dom told her when she'd cut the car's motor. "My grandfather used to come here. By the time I was a kid, it was already closed down, but we came out anyway, mostly to sit by the river in peace. You know, away from everything. Now I come by myself. I've never seen anyone else here. Never brought anyone, either."

Caitlin took in the significance of his bringing her here today.

"Come on," he said, leaning across and pushing open her door, then his own. "Let's see about this lunch." He opened the sagging screen door of the lodge and went inside, emerging a few minutes later carrying a green wooden table. He set it in the middle of the clearing, under the leaves of a tree that dappled the sunlight onto the ground beneath it. A second trip inside netted one and a half chairs. That is, he came out with one wooden chair and another that was really just a seat with three legs attached.

"I'll take this one," he said and sat down at the table, indicating with a wave that she should do the same.

Caitlin laughed. "I couldn't ask for more elegant surroundings."

She opened the basket and started setting out the lunch.

"Boy," he said, opening the foil around one of her and Esther's sandwich masterpieces — tuna salad with tomato and bacon and swiss cheese.

"What'd you think?" she teased. "That I was going to bring bread and water?"

"Well, no, but peanut butter maybe." He held up one of the red-checkered napkins by a corner, letting it fall open, as if to illustrate his point. "Maybe I've just at sea roughing it for too long."

"What's it like?" she asked. "On a ship?"

"Oh, at first it's exciting. After a while, though, it's like being in a small can in a big bathtub. Maybe that's why I took the job at the club. It had the most earth and grass to it of anything I could find."

"But you must've really seen the world in those two years."

"I saw a lot of port towns, which isn't exactly seeing the world."

"You make it sound like a total drag."

He shook his head. "No, it was a lot of experiences. I still haven't sorted them all out. You know, like a box of photos before you get them pasted down in an album."

While they ate lunch, he told her about some of the places he'd seen. France, Spain, Italy, Greece, Australia, Hong Kong. He wasn't a smooth, easy talker like Jennifer's boyfriend, Alan, but he wasn't the monosyllabic Neanderthal Caitlin used to think Dom, like his friends, was. A guy who could only talk about car engines and girls and how much beer he'd drunk the night before.

One surprise was how much he thought about his family. There were two younger brothers and a sister after him and Patti. The way he talked, he and Patti felt responsible to stay home and help their parents financially with the little ones. She wondered why Patti had never mentioned this to her.

When they'd eaten and then sat talking for what seemed like ten minutes, but was probably an hour, he said, "I thought we were going to go swimming."

"But," Caitlin said, looking around, "where are we going to change?"

"Well . . . do mice bother you?"

"You bet!"

"Girls," he said, shaking his head. "Okay then, I'll go change in the lodge. You give a shout when you're ready out here."

"How do I know you won't cheat and look?"

"You could blindfold me but, really, I think you're just going to have to trust me."

The straight-on way he looked at her made her know she *could* trust him, not just in this silly way, but in bigger ones, too. When he'd disappeared into the lodge, she hung her shorts and T-shirt on a low branch of one of the trees and wriggled into her suit, then called out to him as she ran down the clay bank and into the clear, blue water. No matter how hot the summer, the river held onto its stunning chill. Almost everyone hit the water with a brief scream — a mix of astonishment and delight.

"Eeeeeahhh!" went Caitlin, no exception to the rule. Dom followed a minute later and dove under for so long and so deep she couldn't find him until he surfaced directly in front of her, his body brushing hers as he came up for air.

This completely demolished Caitlin's plan, which had been for them to have this little picnic, then sometime this week a night date — to the movies out at the mall, she'd thought — where he'd put his arm around her. Then a third date, and at the end of that one, they'd have their first kiss. And so she was totally unprepared for Dom, at this too-much, too-soon moment, pulling her to him, their bodies clinging to each other like sea ferns beneath the water's surface, their slightly blue lips touching so suddenly and then pressing so passionately that Caitlin finally understood the meaning of the word "breathless."

Chapter 6

Sunday night, Jennifer and Alan were baby-sitting for her brother, Scotty. "Monster-minding," Alan called it. The three of them had just finished watching a video of *King Kong*, the original black-and-white version, which Jennifer thought was superior to the remake, "even with all its technical advances."

"This is what I'm in for," Alan told Scotty. "Years and years of expert opinions. And she's not even in college yet. Imagine what she'll be like by the time she's in grad school."

"She's always had strong opinions, even when she didn't know anything," said Scotty, who wanted to rewind the video and watch the movie all over again.

"No way, José," Jennifer told him. "It is my solemn monster-minding duty to have you in bed by nine, and you're already an hour past that. If Mom and Dad come home and find you still up, they'll probably fire me and bring in Mrs. Harris, even though she hates night jobs."

"You guys just want me to leave so you can make out."

"No," Alan said, "we can just make out with you right here. No problem." With that, he grabbed Jennifer into a hug and big kiss.

"I'll go! I'll go!" Scotty shouted, running out of the den and up the stairs and then back down again to hug Alan, then up again for good.

Jennifer got up off the couch and began clearing away the empty soda cans and bowls of cheese curls and chips. Alan helped, following her into the kitchen.

"I can't wait to have our own monsters," he said, putting his arms around her from behind as she stood at the sink.

"Oh, Alan," she said, turning to face him. "Me, too. Well, maybe not monsters quite so monsterly as Scotty, but yes, yes, I definitely want to, too. But that seems light years away, doesn't it? I mean first we have college to get through, and then I'll have grad school and you'll have med school and then an internship, then a residency. My parents didn't stop long enough to have me until they were almost in their thirties. Thirty just seems impossibly far off, doesn't it?"

"Yeah," he said, his tone changing slightly. "Especially now that it's not such a sure thing I'll even *make* it to thirty."

"Alan! Stop talking like that. It creeps me out."

"I'm going to have the test."

"Why?! You're just driving yourself crazy with imaginary illnesses you don't even have."

"No. It wasn't my idea. Stoddard wants me to have it." Jim Stoddard, an internist in practice with Jennifer's father, was Alan's doctor.

"Oh, well," Jennifer said, trying to get her mind around this huge, threatening thing she couldn't even identify. "It *is* just a test. They just want to make sure you *don't* have it. Jillions of people get tested for jillions of reasons . . ."

He cut off her nervous babbling by gripping both her arms and looking at her dead-on. "I think I have it."

"You're just being pessimistic because you don't want to jinx it by being too optimistic. I do that kind of thing myself all the time," Jennifer answered nervously.

"No! I know because I know how I feel, test or no test. And how I feel is rotten. I feel like somebody took away my body and left me one of an eighty-year-old man. Something's wrong." He stopped for a moment, then said in a soft voice, almost a whisper, "I'm scared, Jen."

Chapter 7

"Three club sandwiches, hold the mayo on one, and a grilled cheese!" Patti shouted through the service window to the grill's kitchen. It was a quarter to one and her feet were already aching from running nonstop to keep the lunchtime diners at Hickory Hills happy. As hard as the job was on her feet, it was even harder on her ego. It was one thing to serve the adult members. She even got a kind of kick out of showing them she was capable and efficient at her job. But she was really frosted at what had happened when Jennifer and Caitlin had come in earlier, around eleven-thirty. They ordered BLTs and iced coffees. (The two of them always ordered the same thing when they were together. They'd done this since they were little.)

Of course they'd said hi to Patti and goofed around with her a little when she came over to take their orders. It wasn't as though they'd disowned her because she was now just a waitress, while they were members. Nothing as blatant as that. It was more that her waitress status had made her invisible, made her disappear to her old friends, replaced by someone in a nylon uniform bearing sandwiches and beverages.

When she came out with their orders, Jen and Cait were deep in conversation, clearly about something important. (She could always tell by the way their heads were lowered, their voices quiet.) But whatever it was that had made them so serious, got dropped as soon as she started setting their plates on the table. The two of them became silent, then politely thanked her when she was done. It was this politeness that was the weirdest part, the part that made it feel like there was suddenly this huge chasm between them and her.

And, she thought on her way back to the kitchen with her empty tray, what could they possibly be talking about that they'd want to keep from her? She'd felt this same way on Saturday when she brought their drinks out to the pool. It was as though her worst fears were coming true already — the other rain dancers had left high school behind and now were leaving her in the same dust.

"What's got you so down?" Danny asked when the lunch crowd had thinned out and there was a pause in the kitchen action.

"Nothing," Patti said.

"You're a terrible liar," he said.

"Oh, well, it's just that I feel like I'm becoming a nonperson in this waitress uniform. I feel like my old friends just see me as the person bringing the Cokes and sandwiches now. And it's only going to get worse. What happens when you all come home from school on breaks? You'll have all sorts of common experiences and stuff to share and laugh about, and what part will I be able to have in all that? I'll be able to say, 'I really served a lot of tuna salad bowls last week.' "

"You're taking a small thing too seriously. If you go to the library this summer, you'll have to ask Leah to help you find a book. If you wind up in the hospital, Jennifer will have to carry your bedpan."

They imagined this scene and cracked up at the same time.

"Okay, okay," Patti said, giving Danny a hug. "I'm lucky to have you as a friend," she told him. "You always help me put things in perspective."

"Think nothing of it," he said, then held out his hand, palm upward. "Now, that will be fifty dollars for the psychiatric consultation, please."

It was only a couple of minutes later that Patti felt a looming presence behind her as she was counting up her tips for the lunch shift. She turned and looked over her shoulder to find Brice Fraser standing there, just watching her. He was wearing wild print pants and his stupid red and green bowling shoes. He wore these nearly all the time, as though they were some kind of bold personal statement, when really they just attracted snide comments around school.

"Something I can do for you?" she asked him.

"Well," he said in a slithery, insinuating tone. "I couldn't help overhearing, and I just want you to know I'm on your side."

"My side of what?"

"I think they're a bunch of jerks, too. Your so-called friends."

Patti felt an instant rage surge through her. "Brice, I'm not on your side of anything. What you overheard was a private conversation. It's none of your business."

"Okay, okay!" Brice said, throwing up his hands. "Just trying to be friendly. Or don't you bother being friendly with anyone outside of your precious little clique?"

This stung her. Although the other rain dancers were her closest friends, Patti made a point of being friendly to everyone. If there was one thing she wasn't, it was a snob.

"Brice, just what is it you want?"

"Well, for a start, maybe we could catch a movie Saturday night."

"Uh, I don't think so," she said, fumbling desperately for an excuse. She tried to duck out by pushing through the swinging doors into the grill's dining room. There were very few members still eating. She picked up a pot of coffee and began to make a round of filling everyone's cup. At the closest table were Doc McPherson and Will Oakley, the owner of Oakley's, the biggest department store in the mall. Both were cronies of Brice's father.

Brice just followed her right over to their table.

"So how about it?" he asked, making it seem as though he and Patti were in the middle of a conversation, instead of at the end of it.

"How about what?" she said, bewildered.

"Going out with me Saturday night?"

"Oh," she said. "I'd love to, but . . ."

"But you're washing your dog," Brice said, much to the amusement of Doc and Mr. Oakley, who started chuckling.

"Uh, well . . ." Patti said. (*Brilliant*, she thought. *Am I smooth, or what?*)

"Oh, go on," Mr. Oakley said. "Say yes."

"That's right," Doc said. "Let the poor guy off the hook. Don't leave him twisting in the wind."

With all this good-natured prompting, Patti knew she would look like a witch if she turned Brice down.

"Oh, all right, then," she said, not particularly graciously; but getting a yes at all seemed to satisfy Brice and his rooting section.

"Great," he said, breaking into a smile that made her feel bad for not wanting to go when it clearly meant so much to him. "I'll come by for you at seven, then."

"Fine," she said, thinking maybe he wasn't as bad as he seemed. In sophomore and junior years, Patti had gone out with Tim Finnegan but, since they'd broken up, there hadn't been a boyfriend prospect in sight. Not that Brice was a prospect, but this would be the first date she'd had in a long time. Maybe it would at least be an okay evening. Maybe.

Leah got off from the library at four. Her first day had actually been more fun than she'd expected. First, it was nice hanging out with her mother.

After her parents were divorced three years earlier, Leah's mom had gone back to being a librarian. Since she was on the late shift, from one in the afternoon until the library closed at nine, Leah didn't usually get to see much of her during the week.

That was hard, because they'd become a lot closer since the divorce. Her mother had begun confiding in her — about their finances, her own feelings. When they moved — after Leah's dad had left to be with Janine, a paralegal at his law firm who was only five years older than Leah — her mom asked Leah to help choose and then decorate the town house they rented. Leah felt they were friends now besides being mother and daughter.

Still, she hadn't been looking forward to this job at the library. She thought it would just be a lot of shelving books and checking them out. But even this first day, she'd had more interesting things to do. She had decorated the new summer window display, "Take a Vacation with Books." Then, in the afternoon, her mother asked Leah to do the Reading Circle for little kids, reading to them from a book about a family of mice. She couldn't believe how much they got into it, laughing like crazy at the funny parts and squiggling in their tiny chairs during the exciting parts.

"It looks like you're a natural actress," her mother told her afterward, "doing all those different voices. You were really a performer."

This gave Leah a great idea. If she was such a good actress, she ought to be able to make Greg

Wright believe she was drowning. Then he'd have to notice her, pay attention to her, take her into his arms. She let her mind run free imagining the scene.

"Help! Help!" she would shout in a voice filled with fear.

Greg's head would turn sharply as he was alerted to her distress and, with one fluid movement he would whip off his visor and swan-dive into the pool, coming up behind her and wrapping a tanned, muscled arm across her. As he pulled her along, out of the deep end and over to the side, her head would be nestled between his arm and his chest. And in this moment, something about Leah's vulnerability would make him look at her in a new way, a way he never had before, a way that made him press his slightly sun-chapped lips against hers and forget all about Shannon Christopher.

In reality, the scene turned out quite differently.

The pool wasn't very crowded when she emerged from the women's locker room late that afternoon. There were a few little kids playing in the shallow end and a couple of junior high boys doing cannon-balls off the high dive. Keeping a serious eye on all this was Greg, his nose white with zinc oxide, the rest of him nut brown and slightly shiny with tanning oil.

He didn't pay any particular attention to Leah as she left her towel on a chaise and stepped out of her sandals, diving off the side into the deep end of the pool. She stayed under as long as she could, then figured it was now or never. She thrust herself upward, bursting out of the water with a scream.

"Help! Help!" she shouted, then coughed and sputtered and flailed her arms wildly, to give her "drowning" a realistic look. Then she went down again, and from underwater she could see the form of Greg Wright plunging toward her.

And then he had one arm across her chest and in a strong, serious voice was saying, "Just stay calm. Just relax. Let me do all the work. You're fine now." This part was just like her fantasy. It felt wonderful, his arm across her, her head resting on his chest, which was warm and smelled like cocoa butter.

And then the dream suddenly took a sharp turn into reality. She felt herself being hoisted from Greg's hands into those of Ray Crawford, the other lifeguard on duty, a heavyset guy with a really bad acne problem. Next thing she knew, she was flat on her back with Ray and Greg hovering over her. She kept her eyes shut.

"Think she needs mouth-to-mouth?" she heard Greg say.

"Maybe," she heard Ray say.

"Well," Greg said, "you're the expert at it. Go ahead."

Her plan was backfiring. The last thing on earth she wanted was mouth-to-mouth resuscitation with Ray Crawford's lips on her own, his acne bearing down on her. She opened her eyes instantly.

"Ah, I think she's okay," Greg said. Then, looking intently at Leah, he asked her, "Are you?"

She nodded and then said in a whisper, trying to sound like someone just back from a near brush with the hereafter — kind of like Julia Roberts in *Flatliners* — "I think so."

"Great," Ray said.

"Yeah," Greg said, helping her to her feet. "You just took in a little water, Linda."

Linda? she wailed inside. Here she was drowning to get his attention, and she'd only succeeded in nearly getting herself mouth-to-mouthed by Ray Crawford and finding out that after an entire school year in the same English class, Greg Wright hadn't even got her name right. Argh!

Chapter 8

Caitlin steathily tiptoed across her bedroom to the closet. She slipped inside and shut the door behind her before turning on the light. She didn't want her parents, whose room was across the house's central courtyard, to see her light going on and get suspicious.

She had just gotten off the phone with Dom. They had talked every night since Sunday. Maybe "talked" wasn't exactly the right word for what they did. A lot of the time, the connection between them was something that came through silence. Dom was not a big talker, but that didn't seem to matter. Somehow, between them, talking seemed almost irrelevant.

Tonight, neither of them had wanted to hang up.

"I've got to see you," he finally said. Caitlin had been trying to cool things down a little by waiting until the weekend, but nothing was getting cooler, not the temperature in River Bend, nor the temperature between her and Dom.

"When?" she said.

"Now."

"Dom! It's after midnight. My parents are sleeping — and they're both *light* sleepers — just across the way from me."

"Just sneak out. They're not going to miss you. I'll be waiting at the end of your drive in twenty minutes." When she didn't say anything, her mind racing with ambivalence and contradiction (scared and thrilled at the same time), he whispered, "Please." And hung up.

She decided that for a night escape, she should dress like a cat burglar. She put on a pair of black jeans, a black T-shirt, and black high-top tennis shoes, and crept down the front stairs, which were thickly carpeted. There was no window in the front entrance hall, so she didn't even have the moonlight to guide her. She was walking as softly as she could across the tile floor when suddenly there was a terrible *"Rrrreeeooooowwww!!!"*

She'd stepped on the tail of Tickle, their cat, who must have been asleep on the cool tile.

Caitlin stood as still as a statue and waited for one or the other of her parents to come roaring out of the bedroom to find her, know instantly what she was up to, and ground her until she was twenty-five.

But they didn't.

She moved to the front door, pressed the code on the security system panel, and slipped outside. Immediately, she was hit by a wall of heat. This hot spell and Dom were all tangled up inside her in ways she couldn't quite understand. The heat made her want to get out of her clothes and under a cold shower in much the way that her feelings about Dom made her want to be back in the river with him, their bodies cool and slippery in the water.

She had replayed that kiss in her mind a hundred times in the days since — the days she'd put off seeing him; afraid, not of him, but of the new feelings inside herself. Feelings that were burning higher than the still black air of this midnight.

When she got to the end of the drive, she saw his pickup truck. He was leaning against it in jeans and an old white shirt, unbuttoned and falling open in front, the sleeves rolled up unevenly above his elbows. His hair was wet, as though he'd just taken a shower to try to cool down, chill out.

"Hi," she said, then once again felt out of breath, the way she had in the river.

He smiled, as if seeing the effect he was having on her. When she was close enough, he reached out and, with just the tips of his fingers, touched the side of her face, pulling her hair behind her ear.

"Let's go somewhere," he said. "Let's go to the club."

"The club?"

"Yeah. There's a place there I like."

"I'll bet I know where you mean," she said, and saw she was right when they got to the club and took the service road in behind the fourteenth hole. Surrounding the green was a water hazard, a man-made pond with gently sloping banks.

"My handiwork," he said as they sat down on the

73

incline. "I mowed every blade of this grass today."

"Just for me?" Caitlin teased.

"Of course. I let the members think it was for them, though."

Caitlin smiled and watched Dom lie back onto the slope, his fingers interlocked behind his head. She leaned back beside him.

"You can see every star tonight," she said. "When I was little, my dad got me a telescope and taught me all the constellations. So, if you'd like a guided tour . . ."

"Sure," he said, shifting around on the grass a bit, like an audience settling in for a performance.

"Well, that's Cassiopeia over there," she said, pointing.

"Over where?"

"There, next to the Little Dipper."

"I can't even see the *Big* Dipper," he said, grabbing the hand she was pointing with and holding it to his chest, over his heart.

"You're hopeless," she said.

He propped himself up on an elbow, facing her, his white shirt luminescent in the moonlight, falling open onto the thin strip of space between them.

"No," he said, now very serious. "Right now, I'm hope*ful*."

"About . . . ?"

"About the possibility of someone like you falling in love with someone like me."

"Dom, you're not someone like you. You're you. And I'm me. Not types. Just two tiny specs in the universe."

He pulled her up to him, and they began kissing, slowly at first, then faster. Mouth on mouth, then on necks and ears, hands running through hair, and then — not as though they were crossing a line, but as though everything that was happening was inevitably along the same continuum — they were tugging off each other's shirts.

"Dom," Caitlin heard herself say, or rather some part of herself that was holding onto some measure of sense and composure. "We'd better stop."

Later that same night, around two A.M., Jennifer came out of one of the rooms on her floor of the hospital.

"Bed Two in three-forty needs more pain meds," she told Ellen Schaefer, the head nurse on duty. "He's climbing the walls." The man in Bed Two, Room 340, had been through gall bladder surgery earlier that day and was in a lot of post-op pain.

Before Jennifer started working at the hospital, she expected the hardest part of the job to be carrying bed pans and emptying catheter pouches and dressing wounds. All the gross stuff her friends teased her about in advance. When it came down to it, though, none of these things fazed her.

"You must have a cast-iron stomach," Florence, the other aide on the floor, said after Jennifer had been subjected to a night of the goriest and grisliest stuff the hospital had to offer.

The hardest part — which Jennifer hadn't really given much thought to in advance — was seeing people die. So far, in these first days on the job, two patients on the floor had died. Mrs. Kirby in 327, of cancer. Mr. Edson in 332, who had been admitted after an accident in the oil fields where he worked, died just after he'd come out of intensive care.

Both times, it was startling to Jennifer that someone who'd been alive just moments before — groggy with pain meds or weaving in and out of consciousness, maybe, but alive all the same — could now be stiffening and going cold, a body, a corpse to be cleaned and zipped into a paper shroud and put onto a gurney, then wheeled into the elevator for its descent to the basement morgue.

And now, down at the end of the corridor in the AIDS section, a third patient was dying. Since the night Jen started, this patient — Richard Everett — had been her favorite. In spite of how gravely weakened he was with the multiple infections assaulting his faulty immune system, in spite of the most recent development — total blindness — he held on to his sense of humor. Through the tubes feeding him and helping him breathe and monitoring his vital signs, he managed to joke about it all.

"I think there's a call for you on my switchboard," was the first thing he'd said to Jen when she'd come into the room and been stopped cold by all these tubes and wires.

She couldn't believe she was standing next to a dying man and cracking up.

"I'm sorry," she had said.

"Why? You should only feel bad if you *don't* laugh at my jokes."

Tonight, when she'd come on at eleven and been briefed by the head nurse from the previous shift, Jen had been told that this would probably be Richard's last night.

"And they *always* die at night," Florence said. Florence was a font of nitty-gritty hospital wisdom.

When Jennifer passed Richard's room on the way to take temperature and blood pressure readings on a new admission, she noticed he was all alone.

"Why isn't anyone in there with him?" she asked Ellen Schaefer when she got back to the nurses' station. "Where's his family?"

"We called next-of-kin," Ellen said, "but they shot us down. Apparently they disowned Richard when they found out he's gay. They don't want any part of his suffering."

"That's just so horrible," Jennifer said. "But doesn't he have someone — you know — a friend?"

"His lover died last year," Ellen said. "In this hospital. I first got to know Richard as a visitor. And since he's been here as a patient, he *has* had visitors, but it's hard to watch someone you know die. A lot of bystanders drop away near the end."

"But shouldn't someone be with him now?" Jennifer asked. "I mean, no one should have to die alone, should they?"

"Tell you what," Ellen said, putting an arm around Jennifer's shoulder. "Why don't you get your rounds done, then go in there and keep him company. I'll ask Florence to cover for you in your other rooms."

Jennifer nodded and rushed off to get through her rounds. By one, she was able to start her vigil with Richard. As she sat next to him, he focused in, then dropped away from consciousness, his breathing laborious even with the help of a respirator.

Jennifer had only two thoughts running on a loop through her head. One was the wish that Richard could just die and be free of his terrible suffering. The other was the impossible possibility — that she might be sitting in this very same room sometime, only it would be Alan in the bed, hooked up to all these machines, his pale gray eyes wet with pain. She pressed the thought out of her mind. Alan's test was going to be negative. Negative. Negative.

When Ellen looked in to see how things were going, Jennifer knew she would just assume the tears in her eyes were for Richard. She couldn't guess their other source.

Chapter 9

Patti was blow-drying her hair when Dom came into the bathroom and began looking through the medicine cabinet. He tapped Patti on the shoulder and said something, which got drowned out by the dryer. She turned it off.

"What?"

"I said, did you swipe my after-shave?"

She laughed. "Yeah. I wanted to smell all manly and virile for my big date."

"You have a *date*?"

"I know it's amazing, but it's true."

"With who?"

"That's the bad part. Brice."

"Brice Fraser?"

"As opposed to all the other Brices in town? Of course, Brice Fraser."

"Why would you go out with a geek like that?"

"Because he asked me in front of a dining room full of club members," she said, slightly overstating her case for dramatic effect. "And I couldn't think fast enough on my feet to turn him down."

"Where are you going?"

"To see a movie is what he said. Hey, I'll live through it. It's been so long since I've had any date at all that even with a geek, I might wind up having an okay time."

They both thought about the likelihood of this for a moment, then looked at each other and said simultaneously, "Nah."

"As long as we're being nosy," Patti said when she'd finished drying her hair, working around her brother while he tried to shave in front of the same mirror, "I wonder where you're going tonight that requires all this shaving and after-shaving. Can't be over to Ernie's garage to work on somebody's carburetor."

"Caitlin and I are going out."

"It must be serious," she observed, "the way you've both clammed up about it."

"Yeah," Dom said, "well . . ."

"Mr. Chatterbox," Patti teased, then laughed at a thought that was crossing her mind. "I'd love to see the expressions on Mr. and Mrs. Carney's faces if they found out their daughter was seeing the club greenskeeper."

"Well, they're not *going* to find out. We're making sure of that."

"Oh, Dom, you do seem serious. I hope you know this can only be a summer affair."

"What do you mean?" he asked.

"Well, Caitlin is on her parents' program. In a couple of months, she'll be off to Vassar and a whole new life that won't include people like us."

"Maybe," he said.

"What do you mean, maybe?"

"Just that she has other options."

"Like marrying you and working in the drugstore downtown while you mow lawns, the two of you living in an apartment above the bowling alley with a couple of screaming kids?"

"It wouldn't have to be as terrible as that," he said defensively, as he rinsed off his razor under the tap.

"Get real," Patti said, hanging the dryer on its wall hook. "You are part of Caitlin Carney's present. There is no future tense for the two of you."

"We'll see about that," he said, finally finding his after-shave in the cabinet and splashing some on. "We'll see."

Patti was under the impression that she and Brice were going out to the cinemas at Echo Mall — a Saturday night magnet for kids from Rio Rojo on dates or just in groups of friends. So she dressed up a little (you never knew who you were going to run into there) in her fit-like-a-glove jeans, a purple shirt, and white running shoes. She was a little surprised when Brice showed up (half an hour late) dressed for a pickup football scrimmage in raggy cutoffs and a paint-splotched sweatshirt that looked as though he'd dug it out of the bottom of the laundry hamper. And, of course, he was wearing his red and green bowling shoes. It was instantly clear to Patti that he wasn't overly concerned with making a good impression.

"Hey," he said at the door and looked around for parents he might have to deal with.

"They're out playing pinochle with some friends," Patti told him. "You don't have to behave yourself in front of anyone."

He looked distracted. "Uh, okay. Great. Let's go then."

His Porsche was parked across the street from Patti's house. Why was it, she asked herself, that the worst guys almost always had the best cars?

He didn't bother going around to get the door for her, just shouted lightly, "It's open," as he slid into the driver's seat. When they took off, it was in the direction away from town, rather than toward it and the mall.

"I thought we were going to the movies," she said.

"We are," he said and smiled. "We have a private video screening room. And a library of over a thousand movies. I'm sure we'll have something you like."

Suddenly Patti felt weird. She hadn't counted on spending time all alone with Brice. The thought gave her the whim-whams, even though he didn't seem to be particularly interested in her.

"What . . . ?" she started to say, but he went "Sssshhhh," as he rolled the volume knob up on the radio to catch some baseball scores. Mr. Romantic.

She didn't bother trying to make small talk the rest of the way out to the Fraser place, and neither did he. By the time they got there, Patti was seriously wondering why he'd even asked her out.

It was interesting to see what the Fraser compound looked like from the inside. The house was ultramodern, something you didn't see much around River Bend. The furniture was all black leather. The rooms were red tile with white walls and bold abstract paintings hanging from them. His parents were having some friends over and Brice introduced Patti around.

"We're just going to use the screening room," he said to his father.

"I'd come in and chaperone," his dad kidded, "but I'm busy. Let your consciences be your guide," he added, much to the amusement of his wife and the other couple.

Yech, Patti said to herself. *The mere thought of making out with Brice. Yech.*

The screening room was all gray and carpeted and air-conditioned and windowless. You wouldn't know in there if it were day or night. She looked through a few movies and picked *The Sound of Music* which she knew was a jillion years old and totally cornball, but she loved the songs. She could tell from Brice's pained expression as he popped the tape into the VCR that he was going to really suffer through this. She felt almost gleeful.

They sat on the low gray sofa, as far apart as she could manage without seeming like she was trying to sit in the next room.

"So how are you liking your job at the club?" she said while the camera swooped down those Alps to where Julie Andrews was going to pop over that mountain. "I hear it's supposed to build your character." She thought he would take the tease good-naturedly, but instead he flushed with anger.

"My father's making it a requirement of getting my trust fund. So I'm going along. I've got most of the members wound around my little finger. They're such a pathetic bunch of fogeys and drunks, and the women — all trying to look ten years younger than they are. I act like I think they're gorgeous. You should see my tips. I'll make my dad eat crow. He said I'd never last out a season in a real job. But I will. The only really intolerable part is that — you know, someone like me — should have to work with greaseballs like Danny Sanchez above me."

"Brice, Danny's one of my best friends. I won't sit and listen to your slurring him."

"Yeah, well, forget it then. You clearly don't understand. Besides, it's not Sanchez I want to talk about, it's your friend Caitlin."

"What *about* Caitlin?" Patti said, feeling creepy just hearing Brice mention her name. It was like being Hansel with the Wicked Witch asking you where Gretel was.

"Well, you know, we were dating for a while and kind of drifted apart. Of course, I was busy with a lot of things at the time," he said. Patti had heard quite another version of the two dates Caitlin had had with Brice, but she let him go on. "And now my schedule has opened up a little and I was wondering if you — being her good friend and all — thought she might be interested in picking up where we left off."

"Let me get this straight," Patti said, talking

over the nuns musically wondering "How Do You Solve a Problem Like Maria?" "You asked me out tonight so you could pump me for information on whether Caitlin, with whom you had maybe two dates a couple of years ago, after which she shot you down. Dusted you. Put you in the ejection seat. Whether she would be interested in starting to date you again?"

"Hey. Wait a minute," Brice said, suddenly on the defensive.

"Oh, Brice," Patti said, standing up to leave. "Get a life. No one wants to date you. Caitlin's going with my brother. Every other girl at Rio Rojo is permanently washing her hair as far as you're concerned. And I . . . I believe I'm going home."

And with that, she exited the screening room, and the Frasers' house, and walked the three miles back to town.

Chapter 10

As Patti and Danny were coming on for their lunch shift at the club, there was a notice posted on the bulletin board in the hall by the employee changing rooms.

ALL MALE STAFF MEMBERS
MEET IN CLUB CONFERENCE ROOM
AT 3 P.M. TODAY

"What do you think *that's* all about?" Patti said.

"Oh, probably a competition to see who's the best looking guy at the club," he said. "I will, of course, win hands down. I feel a little sorry for all those poor slobs who'll lose to me."

Danny knew the meeting really had to be about something serious, but he couldn't have guessed *how* serious.

"It has come to our attention," Ken Tyler, the club manager, said when all the guys had arrived at the meeting, "that certain amounts of money have been missing from the lockers in the men's locker rooms. In the entire history of the club, there has never been such an incident. It would simply be unacceptable for our members to have to use locks on their belongings, so this problem must be rooted out at its source and dealt with immediately." Tyler always talked as though he were the head of the CIA rather than just the manager of a country club, as though everything he said was urgent and crucial and authoritative.

All the caddies and kitchen help and greens crew members just stood around the conference room in silence.

"What I'm saying is that we" — Mr. Tyler always used "we" when he actually just meant himself — "expect the perpetrator of these pilferings to come forward, either now, or in my private office. Today. So that a black cloud of suspicion does not linger for long over the entire male staff."

And that was it. No one, of course, stepped forward. Tyler was dreaming, Danny thought. If someone was slimy enough to pick pockets, he wasn't also going to be noble enough to turn himself in.

Danny looked around the room. He knew most of the guys there, and none of them seemed like a crook or even a shady character. Except Brice, who was leaning against the back wall with a stupid smirk on his face, as if this sort of meeting was beneath him. It *could* be Brice. Even though he was richer than all the other members put together, he did really hate working here, and he made no secret of despising most of the members. He might have done it just out of spite. Danny sidled up to him as everyone was leaving.

"So you've got a little case of sticky fingers, eh Sanchez?" Brice said, smiling with a false sweetness.

"I was just thinking the same about you," Danny came back at him.

"Oh, Danny boy, believe me, I wish I were the culprit. I wish I'd been the one to think up such a devilish scheme. I would love to be the thief and get myself fired and have a beautiful summer around the home pool, keeping an eye on our new upstairs maid, Juanita. She comes from your native land. The land of jumping beans and colorful dances around hats."

"My native land is America, you stupid jerk, but that doesn't mean I'm not proud of my Mexican background," Danny said, then shoved his hands in his pockets to keep himself from hauling off and slugging Brice.

He wished Brice *had* turned out to be the thief, but if it was true that getting fired was what he most wanted, then stealing from the members would only get him out of a job he hated, and he would have already "confessed" to Tyler. Danny hoped they found whoever it was, soon. He knew from his family's restaurant business that it was bad having a thief around. Everyone else felt they were under suspicion. In this case, Danny supposed he himself was being watched carefully, too, and he didn't like the feeling one bit.

Jennifer woke up a little after two in the afternoon to the pulse of the phone ringing. (She had adapted herself to the night shift by sleeping from eight in the morning until two in the afternoon, then living her life between two and ten-thirty, when she had to leave for the hospital.)

It was Alan.

"Hey," she said.

"Hey to you, too," he said. He sounded odd, as if this was a conversation with a point to it, instead of the usual calls they had, which had no point whatsoever except to keep the conversation between them strong and constant.

"Are we going out tonight?" she said, still foggy.

"I can't tonight. My Aunt Gertrude is in town. I think I told you. Mom's making a big dinner. You can come if you want."

"Is your Aunt Gertrude the one who pinches everyone's cheek and says how much they've grown and likes to hold after-dinner spelling bees?"

"Yep. It's *that* Aunt Gertrude."

"I think I'll pass," Jennifer said. "We can do something extra fun tomorrow night. To make up for the spelling bee."

"You're on," he said, and laughed, but it was a forced chuckle. "Listen, there's something . . ."

"Hold on," she told him. "I've got a call coming in on call waiting." She clicked the button and found Caitlin on the other end. "Hang on," she told her.

"I'm on with Alan, but we were just winding up."

When she got him back on the line, she said, "It's Cait. Sounds like something important." She wasn't sure why she was lying. She just knew she wanted to get away from Alan and his problems, she just couldn't handle them at the moment.

"So," she teased Caitlin when she was back on the line with her. "How come I'm not seeing my best friend as much as I used to?" This was mostly a tease. She and Caitlin had, of course, just gotten together for lunch at the club a few days before. But there was an undercurrent of truth to her remark. Now late at night, Caitlin was on the phone with Dom, not Jennifer.

"Well, uh . . ."

"Oh, Cait. Don't feel guilty about abandoning your friends in favor of your lustful desires."

"It's not about sex," Caitlin said and, when there was a long pause on the other end of the line, she conceded, "Well, it's not *just* about sex."

"So," Jennifer said. "Are you busy tonight? You want to have dinner with me at Pizza Joe's before I have to go to work? Alan's busy, so why don't you and I go out and celebrate your new, uh, extracurricular activity? You can tell me all the juicy details."

"I'll only come if I don't have to tell you *any* juicy details," Caitlin said, laughing.

"Okay, come and I'll drag them out of you in subtle ways. And the dinner's my treat. This is my first real job, and even though the pay's not that great, this cash is burning a hole in my pocket."

"How can I turn down an offer of free pizza?" Caitlin said and they planned to meet at seven.

Pizza Joe's was located near Rio Rojo and was a big hangout for high school kids in River Bend. But tonight was an off night and Caitlin and Jennifer asked Louise, their favorite waitress, for a booth in the back — in case anyone came in. They both had reasons for wanting this to be a private conversation.

They looked over the menus for a long time and then finally ordered a large, thin-crust pizza with double cheese, black olives, and onions — the same pizza they wound up ordering every time they came to Pizza Joe's.

"Hey, did Alan hear about his test?" Caitlin asked. "I mean does he know if he's positive, or negative? I forget which is which. I mean, does negative mean he flunked?"

The last time they'd really talked — over lunch at the club grill, trying not to let anyone else, not even Patti, hear — Jennifer had told Caitlin that Alan was going to be tested for AIDS.

"No, in this case, negative is good. It means he doesn't have the virus. And no, he hasn't heard yet. At least he hasn't told me if he has." She didn't mention how she'd cut him off on the phone today even though he sounded like there was something he wanted to tell her. She wasn't even sure why she'd done that.

"Well, whatever he has, I hope he gets over it pretty soon. Lately he's been looking so much worse and all . . ."

"What do you mean?" Jennifer said.

"Well, he just does, is all. So pale, and he must've lost twenty pounds. Jen, you *have* to have noticed. He's like a shadow now, like he's fading away."

They were interrupted by Louise setting the pizza down between them and kidding around with them, wondering how two skinny girls were going to eat such a huge pizza. Jennifer decided to put Caitlin's comments out of her mind. Alan might look worse, but he was getting better. And he *didn't* have AIDS. When the test results were back, they'd be negative.

"So," she said to Caitlin, steering the conversation onto a happier subject, "what's been going on between you and the suddenly gorgeous Mr. Costa?"

"He *is* beautiful, isn't he?" Caitlin said in a dreamy way. "It's not just me being deluded?"

"Oh, I guess he's okay if you go for hunky guys with smoldering eyes and curly black hair and iron-pumping bods," Jennifer teased. "But what — and I don't mean to be rude here — what do the two of you find to talk about? I mean, it's hard to see this as a great meeting of minds. The Dom Costa I remember was not exactly Mr. Intellect and Cultural Events."

"Well, I guess we don't talk all that much," Caitlin admitted. "It's more an all-over being with him thing that I like. He's easy for me to feel close to.

I've never really had that with a guy. Actually, this whole thing is a new experience for me, being liked just for who I am, as opposed to being liked for what I can do. For being smart and a good girl, for getting good grades. He doesn't care about any of that. He just likes me with no conditions attached." She stopped and smiled and pulled a cheese-stringy piece of pizza away from the pan, then added, "Plus he kisses incredibly. *In*credibly."

"But what're you going to do come fall?" Jennifer wondered. "I mean it sounds like you've already lost your head over him. What if you lose your heart, too?"

Caitlin nodded, really listening to what Jennifer was saying. Then she replied, "I guess the truth is, for once I'm *not* thinking ahead. I've been like a mini-adult for years now. I feel like I missed out on just being a regular teenager. So now I'm going to do just that, just live for *now*."

"Well, I don't want to burst your balloon. Really. And it's great seeing you so carefree. I don't think you've had a chance to be carefree since about fifth grade."

"I know," Caitlin said. It was true.

"But whether you want to see them or not, there are going to be consequences to something like this. I just want you to be okay when September comes."

"September's a long way away," Caitlin said. "But thanks, Jen. You're the first person I've even talked to about me and Dom. I've been afraid."

"Because he's different?"

Caitlin nodded.

"I know what you should do!" Jennifer said and realized too late that she was squealing. "Bring him to the fireworks Saturday night."

The rain dancers had planned to meet in back of the high school, where the town's Fourth of July fireworks show was put on every year. Going to this together was one of their long-standing traditions.

"Oh, boy," Caitlin said, "I don't know."

"Oh, come on. It'll be an easy way for him to get to know everyone. If he's not talkative, he can just watch the show. It won't be like he's on the spot or anything. And he's not just your boyfriend, he's Patti's brother. So he'll already be comfortable with two of you, and I promise to be manning the welcome wagon."

Caitlin laughed at the image of Jennifer and her welcome wagon.

"I'll ask him," she said. "He might say no, though. He might want to be alone, just the two of us."

"I think what you need is to not be quite so alone for once. Let some air in. If he's as heated up as you are, you two could spontaneously combust if you don't watch out. You'll wind up on the cover of one of those supermarket newspapers. You wouldn't want that."

Caitlin was laughing. "You mean COUPLE OVERHEATS, BLOWS ITSELF UP?"

Jennifer nodded. "And the little headline underneath the picture of your rubble and ashes will go, BYSTANDERS SAY 'WE THOUGHT THEY WERE PART OF THE FIREWORKS SHOW.' "

Both of them were laughing, but under her laughter Caitlin was worried about bringing Dom into her normal, everyday life. So far, everything between them seemed like a fantasy. Would their romance weather the transfer to reality?

July

Chapter 11

Jennifer looked up at the clock on the wall of the third-floor nurses' station. It was almost three A.M. Working nights was starting to give a weird shape to her life. It was as though the nights were dreams, but the kind of dream that was in sharper focus than her real daytime life. Her days — over at the club, or at the mall, or hanging around her house with Scotty, or at Alan's listening to his jazz CDs — had begun to seem a little trivial and blurry. At night, here in the hospital, everything was clear and important. Life or death. Sick or well. Babies being born, old people dying (along with some not-so-old people like Richard Everett, who had slipped out of his life at five-thirty in the morning, at the end of the long night Jennifer had put in at his bedside).

She felt as though she was growing up fast here, being thrown into the deep end of the real world.

"Would you mind keeping an eye on things for half an hour or so?"

Jennifer looked up, startled out of her thoughts.

It was Ellen Schaefer, head nurse on the shift.

"There's a procedures meeting of all floor nurses. You can page me if anything gets hairy up here. Just don't do any open heart surgery without calling first."

"Okay," Jennifer said, smiling. She liked Ellen, who in turn thought it was a shame Jennifer was set on becoming a filmmaker. ("You'd make a great nurse or doctor," she often said, shaking her head, as though Jennifer were making a big mistake.)

This was the first time Jennifer had been left in charge of the floor. She scanned the panel of call lights. They were all dark, which meant everyone was asleep. No one needed meds or a change of bedding, or comfort after a nightmare.

To the right of the call board was a computer terminal plugged into the hospital's mainframe. Jennifer was a computer freak, an interest that kind of ran alongside her interest in video. She had to admit she was a total techie. She'd taken every computer-related course at Rio Rojo. She loved how being curious was a big asset in using computers (not always true in the rest of life), how if you poked around long enough, you could usually make the computer do what you wanted it to do, give you what you wanted.

She started noodling around on the keyboard, pulling a menu of data categories. She looked down the list.

PATIENT FILES/CURRENT

PATIENT FILES/PAST

SURGERY/INPATIENT

(She pulled up this list and found both her parents.)

TESTS/INPATIENT
TESTS/OUTPATIENT

Outpatient tests? That would be Alan. She called up the list.

PATIENT#? the screen asked her. How could she know what Alan's patient number was? And then she remembered something. She pulled her backpack out of the locker in the medicine room behind her and found a scrap of paper in the bottom. It was a silly poem Alan had written for her while waiting at the hospital a few weeks ago for a chest X ray after one of his mysterious viruses.

> *For Jen*
> *Who scores a ten*
> *and gives me a yen*
> *for peanut butter and potato chip*
> *sandwiches on toast.*

He'd written this on the back of the computer invoice Radiology had given him. Up in the left-hand corner, opposite his name, was a number. 15768. She punched it in, and there he was: Hansen, Alan.

She clicked the OPEN box. At first it was hard to make out what the data meant. There were a lot of codes and numbers that didn't mean anything to her. They'd obviously run a lot of tests on those buckets of blood Alan said they took from him. She kept scrolling, and then suddenly there it was — HIV STATUS. She was so sure the test was negative, she actually blinked, like a disbelieving character in a cartoon, when she saw it was followed by POS.

POS. Her mind raced. POS could only mean one thing. Positive. Alan was HIV positive. He had the AIDS virus. Was that what he'd been trying to tell her on the phone? What she'd been too afraid to hear?

She heard the light squeak of rubber soles against linoleum and knew Ellen and the other nurses were coming back from their meeting. She quickly exited Alan's file, and then the TESTS file, and got the screen back to where it was when Ellen had left — MEDS/INPATIENT.

"Nothing major happened, I take it?" Ellen asked, pulling a metal folder out of the slot rack.

"Oh, no" Jennifer lied, "nothing major at all."

The fireworks were to start at eight-thirty. The rain dancers had arrived early so they could have a picnic and hang out before the display got going.

"Did your cook make these?" Leah asked Caitlin, holding up an inscrutable object and turning it over, peering suspiciously at it. "I know my mother couldn't come up with something like this. She thinks *apple pie* is a little on the ethnic side."

Caitlin looked over. "Mmmhmm. Esther made those. Water chestnuts wrapped in bacon."

"Mrrppphhh," Leah said, nodding in a way Caitlin took to mean "Good."

"Here," Danny said, pulling the foil covering off a plate. "Pass these around. They're my world famous Baby Burritos."

"We make the greatest picnics," Patti said. "They should interview us for *Gourmet* magazine. Who else is creative enough to fix a dinner that mixes Alan's burritos and fried rice, Leah's chocolate mousse, Caitlin's bacon-water chestnuts, and Jennifer's hastily thrown together grape salad?"

Patti and Dom had made a pizza from scratch and brought it over in an old carry-out box, so it was still hot, almost.

"Dom, you're definitely an addition to the picnic food chain," Danny said. "When Patti comes by herself, she just brings a bag of chips."

"I do not!" Patti said emphatically. "But I'll admit Dominick is the pizza king in our house."

"Do you toss your flying dough up in the air?" Jennifer asked.

Dominick looked like a bull that had just been stung by a bee — furious and bewildered at the same time. "Unh-unh," he said, shaking his head no, his eyebrows knitting together.

What's his problem? Caitlin thought. Jenny was the gentlest person in the world. She'd only been trying to show Dom he was welcome here, part of the group if he wanted to be. Why was he acting as if she was grilling him like a police interrogator? Why couldn't he just relax and try to fit in, instead of sitting there insisting on behaving like an interplanetary visitor?

Everything about him said "different." His hair was gelled back off his face in a gangster look. And his clothes — why had he worn his hoodiest look tonight? Old jeans and motorcycle boots and a black Harley-Davidson T-shirt. Everyone else was wearing shorts — baggy ones on the guys, stretch shorts on the girls. And oversized shirts, not skintight like Dom's. Why couldn't he just dress *normally*?

Of course, Caitlin realized, if he did, he'd just look like every other guy in town, and when she was alone with him, she wouldn't feel the excitement that came from his being so different and dangerous looking. But if she liked this when they were alone, why did the way he looked and acted bother her when her friends were around?

Danny was quick to see Dom's discomfort, and smoothed over the awkward moment by changing the subject. "Tyler says someone's been lifting cash out of the male members' lockers. We're all under surveillance," he told everyone dramatically.

"Why aren't the other members under suspicion, too?" Leah wondered aloud.

"Because they're too rich," Alan said. "Their own wallets are so heavy, they couldn't possibly carry someone else's around, too."

"But sometimes rich people steal," Caitlin said. "Haven't you ever heard of kleptomaniacs? They just have to keep stealing, even if they don't need any of the stuff they take."

"In that case, they ought to keep an eye on Mrs. Clemens," Patti said. "She ate the dessert of everyone at her table during the bridge luncheon the other day."

Jennifer felt like her body was here, on the edge of this blanket, nibbling one of Caitlin's water chestnuts, but her mind was far, far away. She wanted to put distance between her and her life, between her and Alan. She was flushed with anger at herself for having been so awful to him, shrinking away from him behind a wall of denial. Still, she couldn't bring herself to talk about it yet.

She hadn't gotten any sleep after coming home from the hospital. She just sat in the armchair in the corner of her room, looking down over the backyards of the houses in her part of Hickory Hills, watching the kids playing and adults working in their yards and gardens or sitting peacefully reading the paper. The whole world was going blithely on its way, unbothered by the fact that hers had stopped dead in its tracks because the person she loved most was dying.

When Alan had come by to get her for the fireworks, she tried to act normal, regular, as though everything was the same as it always had been between them. When in fact, everything was turned inside-out, upside-down.

She could barely speak to him on the way over.

Leah and Danny were both talk monsters, which partially covered up the fact that Jennifer wasn't saying anything. Alan noticed, though; she could tell. All through the picnic he'd been looking at her oddly. She was relieved when dusk turned to darkness and the fireworks began and she didn't have to look at him, didn't have to see his thinness and paleness and the careful way he moved for what these were — the look of someone very ill. She'd seen enough of it at the hospital to recognize it. She'd only been blinded to it when she'd seen it in Alan.

When the fireworks were over — she'd hardly seen them — and the rain dancers were folding up their blankets and packing up all the picnic gear, Jennifer let Alan take her hand as they walked together toward the parking lot.

"We're going for a little swim," Danny said, dangling a key in the air. "Want to come?" He'd been an assistant coach for Rio Rojo's swim team the past two years and had hung onto the key for late-night, sneak-in swims at the school pool.

"No can do," Jennifer said. "Got to work." She was glad to have an excuse. Even if she hadn't had to be at the hospital tonight, she was in no mood to have fun or be with other people, not even her best friends.

"What's going on with you?" Alan asked her when they were in his Jeep on their way back to Jennifer's house.

She thought for a minute and then just decided to lay it out. "I was fooling around with the computer at work. I knew your patient number, so I could get through the security and into your file."

"So you found out the bad news," he said.

She nodded.

"Why were you snooping around, looking into my file?" he asked.

"I wasn't snooping. I was just fooling around," she said and then asked herself if this was really true. Had she just been innocently fooling around, or had she really wanted to know something she couldn't let Alan tell her?

Even though they were stopped at a light, he kept looking straight ahead as he spoke. "I really wanted to tell you the other day."

"I know," she said, covering his hand with her own. "And I was so awful, not letting you."

"No," he said. "Don't feel bad. Now that you *do* know, I almost wish you didn't. I wish there was still more time left for you to think of me as your lover, instead of as somebody dying."

"Oh, Alan," Jennifer said, her eyes filling with tears. "Don't you know by now that whatever happens — good or bad — it happens to both of us. You can't take a problem and make it your own. It's mine, too."

"But this isn't just a problem. This isn't something that's going to get solved or just go away."

"Who says? The doctors don't know everything. People are living longer and longer, even though they have the virus. I've been reading up. We'll need to do more research, though. Together. We can ask Leah's mom to look up the latest articles.

We're going to do everything we can. You and I have never been the type to give up. If we have to pump you full of gallons of carrot juice or put you inside a pyramid, we'll do it, because we are going to beat this thing. Not you. *We*."

"Oh, Jen," he said, pulling the Jeep over to the side of the road, pressing his forehead to the top of the steering wheel. "Don't leave me."

She pulled him toward her and folded him in her arms and pressed her face into his neck to breathe him in, to catch his scent, which always reminded her of burning leaves. It was the scent of his being alive.

"I won't," she told him. "Ever."

Chapter 12

"You might as well give up," Danny's kid sister Connie said, watching him comb his hair. "You're not going to get any better looking."

"Come on, Consuela. Help me out. What do you think about my glasses?" he said, taking them off, peering blearily into the mirror. "Should I get contacts?"

Connie hopped onto his bed so she could get behind him and look in the mirror over his shoulder. "Nope," was her final opinion. "I think you are just a glasses type of person."

"Oh, no!" Danny said and then groaned. "It's the truth, isn't it? That's the whole problem in a nutshell. I'm a glasses type of person."

"What problem? What nutshell?" Connie asked. "Hey, where are you going tonight, anyway — all fluffed up like that?"

"The movies. With Leah."

"Oh," Connie said, her tone dropping back to its usual flatness. "I thought maybe you had a *real* date."

Connie didn't know anything about Danny's secret passion for Leah. No one knew, which was a problem in a way. Sometimes he thought he was going to burst, keeping it all to himself.

"Nah," he said to his sister now, keeping her off the track. "Just one of the rain dancers."

He and Leah were supposed to meet out at Echo Mall, in front of the theaters. The movie started at eight-ten, and it was ten to when Danny got there. He stood off to the side, leaning against a pillar, trying to look as cool as possible in his new black pleated pants, suspenders, and a black and white striped T-shirt.

One of his problems in approaching Leah was that they were almost always surrounded by other people — the rain dancers, other friends from school, guys from the swim team, their families. At last, deep into July, he was getting his first chance of the summer to tell her how he felt, to try to persuade her to at least give him a chance to see if something might develop between them. He wasn't sure how he was going to bring this up. He was just hoping there'd be a spot in the evening when he could express himself without a hundred other people around.

Their being alone together tonight was just a happy accident of fate. Patti and Caitlin were supposed to come along, but at the last minute Caitlin's mom had a pair of theater tickets for the River Bend Players she couldn't use and gave them to Caitlin. Patti wanted to see the play, but neither Danny nor

Leah cared. So they were on their own tonight, an evening at the mall cinemas watching what Danny called "mental garbage" — movies filled with guns and car chases and guys jumping onto speeding trains. Leah loved this stuff, too.

While he was waiting for her, a group of kids from school showed up — a bunch of jocks and their girlfriends, including Greg Wright and Shannon Christopher. He nodded hello and wondered what it was that made guys like Greg so devastating to girls. As opposed to guys like himself, who wound up as every girl's best friend.

Finally, at about five after, Leah came rushing through the mall toward the theater. Danny recognized her, even from a distance. Leah was almost always late, so she was almost always rushing to catch up. If she were a cartoon character, she would have been traveling in a little rolling cloud of dust. Her words came tumbling out, nonstop.

"Oh Danny I'm sorry I'm late but somebody didn't show up at the library for work today and I had to fill in for her do you want to get some popcorn?" She hadn't even noticed his clothes, how he had dressed up for her. The house lights were still on when they came inside the theater, looking for seats.

"Oh, wow, there he is!" Leah screamed in a whisper. Of course, she was referring to Greg. "Come on, let's sit where we can get a good view of him." She led them to a pair of seats way off to the side, but just a row behind Greg and Shannon.

"Yeah," Danny said sarcastically, "I wouldn't

want to be distracted from truly important matters by something inconsequential, like the movie."

"Oh, Danny, be a friend will you? I've got this humongous crush on Greg, so just support me, okay?" She yanked his hand to get him to sit down next to her.

They sat in silence for a moment, while Danny ate popcorn and Leah peered around him trying to get a better look at Greg, who was nuzzling Shannon's neck. Mercifully, the lights went down, and the movie began, and Leah was at least slightly distracted by what was happening on the screen.

"I like these *bright* scenes," she whispered to him.

"What do you mean, *bright*?" he asked.

"Well, scenes like this one." The movie's hero was driving a power boat across a mountain lake on a brilliantly sunny day. "They light up the theater so I can see you-know-who better." She nodded toward Greg, who by now was so intertwined with his girlfriend that they were both practically sharing the same seat.

"Doesn't it bother you that he already has a girlfriend?"

"A little," Leah admitted, opening the box of licorice bits they'd bought at the candy counter. "But I think he's going to get tired of her pretty soon. She's great looking, but incredibly boring."

"I wouldn't say Greg is exactly Mr. Fascinating. He rides a motorcycle, and he's a pretty good swimmer. But, that's about the sum of his good points.

I mean the guy wants to be an accountant. He told me once he really likes the music they play in elevators. He likes practical jokes. You know — those phony spilled ink bottles and plastic vomit and sneezing powder."

A loud *sssssshhhhh!!!* came from the row behind them. Leah nodded as though she agreed that Danny should shut up, and so he did.

Midway through the movie, though, he offered her the last of the licorice bits after shaking them out of the box, onto the palm of his hand. When her fingers touched his palm, he closed his hand around hers and held it while he looked at her with an expression he hoped conveyed the way he felt. He waited for her to speak, to acknowledge him in some way.

"Danny, what's wrong? Do you have a stomachache or something?" she said.

He let go of her hand and said, "No, I'm all right."

"Look," she said, peering down the aisle. "Mr. Perfect is going out to the lobby. I think I'm going to just coincidentally buy myself a Coke."

Danny slumped down in his seat, draping his legs over the back of the seat in front of him. "Why don't . . ." he said to Leah as she climbed over him to get to the aisle, "why don't you just stand outside the men's room with a big net and drop it over him when he comes out?"

"Danny! You're no support at all!" Leah said. *SSSSShhhhhhh!*

Danny put his hands over his ears and slunk down

even further in his seat, thinking, *You're a cool operator, Sanchez. There goes your night of big opportunities.*

When Danny brought Leah home, her mother told them, "You have a message. From Jennifer. Alan's in the hospital with pneumonia. Apparently it's serious. They don't know if he'll pull through."

Jennifer had told all the rain dancers a couple of weeks ago that Alan was HIV positive. Everyone was shocked and upset, but at the same time not really surprised. You only had to look at him to know something was terribly wrong.

By the time Leah and Danny arrived at the hospital and then ran up to the intensive care unit, all the other rain dancers were there, along with Alan's parents and his brother and sister.

Jennifer was wearing her yellow and white nurse's aide uniform. She'd been let off her third-floor duty to keep vigil here.

"Can we go in and see him?" Leah asked Jennifer.

"Not now. He's having trouble breathing. They've got a machine giving him oxygen, and the doctors want him to rest as much as possible. They'll tell us if anything changes — for better or worse." Leah noticed how red Jennifer's eyes were, probably from crying, and what deep circles they had beneath them.

"Alan's a real fighter," Danny said. "He really got stomped in the car accident and came through. And he's going to come back from this."

For some reason, this mention of hope made both

Patti and Caitlin begin to cry, as though hearing something even the slightest bit optimistic made them feel more sharply the bleakness of Alan's situation. Dom, who'd come over with his sister, put an arm around each of them.

After a while, with no word from inside the intensive care unit, the group gathered in the lounge became nearly silent. There was really nothing left to say. Alan was a great guy and horrible things were happening to him. It just wasn't fair.

Behind the silence, each of the rain dancer's thoughts were very different.

Caitlin was holding Dom's hand, thinking how unfair it was that everything was ending for Jennifer and Alan while she and Dom were just starting out. She wished they could all be together, at the beginning.

Patti was feeling petty for her gripes and frustration about being left behind by her friends. Looking around now, she realized they would always be there for her if she needed them.

Danny was looking at Leah, thinking how stupid it was for him to hold back telling her how he felt about her. He'd always thought he had all the time in the world to make his moves. And Alan had probably thought he and Jennifer had all the time in the world.

Leah had been dozing on and off through the early hours of their vigil. She woke up in the silent middle of the night to find Danny looking at her in the oddest way.

"What?" she had whispered across the coffee table to the couch where he was sitting.

"Nothing," he'd said, then revised this to, "I'll tell you later."

Now she was sitting here in the cool light of dawn wondering what Danny Sanchez could possibly have to tell her? And what had that goony look been about?

The sun was already beginning to come up when Alan's doctor came in, along with Jennifer's father, who had come earlier to consult with the ICU staff and with Alan's doctor, Jim Stoddard.

"He's out of the woods," Dr. Stoddard said, and you could almost hear a collective sigh of relief pass through the room. "He's breathing on his own and holding steady. It's going to be a while, though, before he can throw a party for all of you, so I'd advise going home and getting some sleep. Come back later today."

On their way down in the elevator, Caitlin gave Jennifer a long, hard hug.

"He's going to be all right," she said, trying to sound reassuring.

Jennifer nodded. "Yes, but for how long? How long until the next time? And which next time will be the last?"

Chapter 13

"Staying in on a Saturday night?" Mrs. Carney, rustling through the den in a swoosh of silk and an invisible cloud of perfume, asked Caitlin, who was lying on the sofa reading *Madame Bovary*. This was part of a summer program she had set for herself — reading all the great classic novels about women.

"Yeah, I'm becoming a social wallflower," Caitlin said and stretched and yawned for good measure. She wanted to look as settled in as a bear going into hibernation. Madame Bovary was deceiving her husband. Caitlin was deceiving her parents.

They were going out to a big party at the club, a benefit for the River Bend Players. Mrs. Carney sat on the board of the theater group, and they had to go to the party whether Mr. Carney wanted to or not. And he *really* did not.

"I wish *I* were staying in," he grumbled as he passed through the den in his tux, but without shoes and with his shirtfront hanging out and open. "Does anyone remember where I put my shirt studs the last time we went to one of these formal bore-a-thons?"

It seemed as though it was taking her parents forever to get their act together and leave. Caitlin surreptitiously glanced at her watch. A little after eight.

"Aren't you going to be late?" she asked her dad as he was rifling through the drawers underneath the bookshelves. Why he thought his shirt studs would be in the den was anybody's guess. He was basically hopeless at finding anything. What he usually did was this — he'd start looking in the dumbest place so someone else would get exasperated enough to look for whatever it was he couldn't find.

"Here they are, Frank," Caitlin's mother shouted as she came down from upstairs, shirt studs in hand.

But then neither of them could find the keys to the Mercedes, and Caitlin's mother refused to go over in her husband's Jaguar. "You have to fold yourself like a card table to even get in that thing. By the time I got out at the club, I'd look like I'd come from the bottom of a duffel bag," she complained.

By the time they found the keys and the notes for Mrs. Carney's speech asking for more support for the local arts community, Caitlin was about ready to push her parents out the front door. But externally she kept her cool.

"Oh, what I'd give for a nice, quiet night in." Her father smiled wistfully as he passed Caitlin on his way out.

Caitlin closed her eyes as she anticipated how

quiet the night was *not* going to be. She waited five minutes after her parents' car was down the drive, in case they'd forgotten something else. Then she reached for the phone on the floor next to her. Dom picked up after one ring. He must have been sitting right by the phone.

"The coast, as they say, is clear," she told him. She figured her parents would be out at least until midnight. They always wound up staying late at these benefit things. Which, if Dom came straight over, would give them about three hours of total aloneness. Of no parentness. No siblingness (a pitfall of being at his place). No mosquitoness (a hazard of nights spent out on the golf course).

"I thought you'd never call," he said.

"I thought they'd never leave," she said.

"Blink, and I'll be there."

She hung up and dashed upstairs to give herself a last-minute once-over. She looked at herself in the mirrored door to her closet. In one way, she looked the same as ever. Her eyes were still green and her hair was still wild, barely tamable; her body was still tall and thin and leggy. She was wearing an outfit she had put on a dozen times (it was one of her favorites) — her most perfect-fitting jeans, a faded terra-cotta polo shirt with the collar flipped up, and pale blue high-top sneakers.

And yet, despite all the familiarity of the girl facing her in the mirror, there was something different. Something about this Caitlin that was new. She looked closer. It was something about the way she was standing that was a little off-center, a little goofy. There was also something at the back of her eyes that was a little brighter, as if she was smiling inside herself. And then it came to her. She was looking at the same person, at Caitlin Carney, but with a difference that made *all* the difference. She was looking at herself in love.

She brushed her hair and teeth and cupped her hand over her mouth and nose, then exhaled to see if her breath was okay. She was incredibly nervous. She went into her bedroom and dug around under her socks in the top drawer. She pulled out one of the condoms she'd bought this week (nearly dying of embarrassment at the checkout) and slipped it into her back pocket. She didn't know how she was going to bring this up to Dom, but she knew she had to. Watching what was happening to Alan had brought the hard realities of sex in the nineties home to her. Dying of embarrassment was better than dying, period.

The doorbell chimed. She almost tripped over Tickle as she dashed down the stairs and threw open the front door.

"Oh," was all she was able to say when she saw him, leaning against a pillar, sinewy in jeans three times as faded as hers, and a gray sweatshirt with the sleeves cut off, the edges of the material curling over his brown, muscle-defined arms. He smelled spicy, like potpourri.

He stepped inside and closed the door behind him, then turned Caitlin around and pressed her against it while they said hello with several long kisses.

Sometimes when the other girls talked about sex, it was as though it was something you did because a guy wanted to and you wanted the guy. But with Caitlin and Dom, it was something she wanted, too. The need to have him, to be physically connected with him, had been building inside her since that first night at graduation dinner. By now the pressure was almost unbearable, in spite of all the distractions she had tried, all the laps in the pool, all the rides she took across the prairie on Honky Tonk. And so both of them knew — although it was an unspoken knowing — what was going to happen tonight. But suddenly, this knowing, added to being in each other's presence, was too much, made them both a little shy, awkward.

"Wow!" he said, looking around. It took Caitlin a moment to realize he meant her house. "Our whole living room isn't as big as your front hall," he said.

"Come, see the rest of the place. I'll give you a tour," she said, trying to keep it light but knowing her voice sounded nervous, higher pitched than usual.

She took him through the dramatic gray and black living room (which had been photographed once for the home section of one of the Houston papers) and the state-of-the-art kitchen her parents had remodeled just last year. From there, she slid open the glass door onto the deck, which stretched out to the lap pool, and beyond that, the floodlights reached the stables.

Upstairs she showed him her parents' room and

its adjacent bathroom with a whirlpool, steam room, and exercise area.

"It's like a little health club!" Dom said, standing behind Caitlin, his fingers resting lightly on her shoulders.

"And this is my room," Caitlin said, flipping on the switch, but staying out in the hall. She didn't want to bring him inside. It would just be too, well, too obvious, too blatant. (*Hi, this is my bedroom and here's my water bed. Yeah, right.*) "We can watch TV down in the den," was what she really said. *Thank goodness for TV*, she thought. "Do you want a soda? And I can zap some popcorn."

"Just relax," he said, turning her around and pulling her face toward his, his fingers moving up the back of her neck, into her hair. Then he backed off, took her hand, and led her down the stairs. "Now, where's this den?"

They flipped through the cable channels, laughing at the dumb stuff for sale on the home shopping channels and at a terrible program on the public access station. No matter how many times they flipped back to it, it was always the same lady, sawing away at her violin. Finally they started mimicking her, sawing away at their own imaginary violins along with her screeching arrangement of "The Yellow Rose of Texas."

They fell backward on the sofa, laughing helplessly. And then, suddenly, they were still lying on the sofa, but they weren't laughing anymore. They stretched out together, and then Dom was looking down into Caitlin's eyes, brushing his lips across her face, kissing her softly at her temples. Slowly. Tonight, everything was happening very slowly.

"When do you think your parents will be home?"

"Midnight at the earliest. Probably later, but at least until then. We have time."

"For what?" he asked, opening his eyes wide, the picture of schoolboy innocence.

Caitlin laughed and ran her fingers through his long, curly hair and said, "I love you, Dom."

"Hey," he teased her, pretending to be insulted, "that's just what *I* was going to say."

"Really?"

"Really. I really love you, Caitlin."

And somehow saying it and hearing him say it took away any last reservations she had about what was going to happen tonight, what was now already happening.

This time, she didn't stop them at taking off each other's shirts. This time was totally different from that night out on the golf course, or from any of the nights they'd parked out at the old canoe camp and stretched out together across the seat of his pickup, the Top 40 station playing low on the radio. In contrast to the way they always seemed to be rushing, not knowing where they were heading, tonight they knew exactly where they were going, and so they went very slowly, taking their time. Turning off the lights. Putting a moody jazz CD on. Undressing each other in the the moonlight silvering in through the French doors.

Their bodies stretched the length of the sofa,

shivered against each other, but not from the air-conditioning.

They began exploring each other slowly, as if they were curious creatures from different planets with language unavailable to them, trying to know and understand each other through touching, tasting, feeling, tangling around each other and merging, meshing, until it was hard for Caitlin to tell where she left off and Dom began. She could hear their breath, coming hard and fast. She could feel their hearts racing against each other.

Afterward, they lay a long time in this silence, which was closer than any talking could be. Caitlin listened as their breath and hearts slowed, giving way to the mechanical sounds of the house. The steady hum of the air-conditioning, the ticking of the clock over the fireplace mantel, the crunch-crunch of Tickle eating some of her biscuits in the kitchen. And then, hours too soon, the sound of a key in the front door lock, the flick of a light switch, and the soles of her parents' shoes on the front hall tiles. And then, "Caitlin! Where are you, honey?"

Chapter 14

"Oh, this is really a worst-nightmare scenario!" Jennifer said as Caitlin flipped her signal before turning into the parking lot of Echo Mall. "Are they grounding you for the rest of your life or something?"

"Worse. I'm never to see Dom again."

"But how can they enforce that?"

"You forget Dom's father works in my dad's oil fields. He's going to have a talk with him about keeping Dom away from me and with his job at stake, I . . . well, you see what's going to happen."

"Oh, that's rotten of them. Really. You're eighteen. You're old enough to make these sorts of decisions for yourself."

"Tell them that," Caitlin said. "To them, I'm still about nine years old."

"I know this is tragic," Jennifer said even as a smile was breaking onto her face, "but I can't help laughing when I imagine the expression on your mother's face when she found her little Merit Scholar on the sofa in a compromising position with the guy who mows the lawn at their country club."

At the mental picture of this, Jennifer started laughing.

"Jen!"

"I can't help myself."

"Anyway, it wasn't *that* bad. I'd gotten into my jeans and shirt by then. Of course, the shirt was on inside-out, and my socks were still crumpled up on the sofa. Argh," she said. She said this every time she remembered last night's scene.

"Where was Dom at this point?" Jennifer asked as they got out of the Miata and began walking toward the stores. "Pretending to be an armchair?"

"When we heard them come in, I told him to grab his clothes and go out the kitchen door in the back. Still, they got the general idea. I mean his truck was parked out front when they came home. As you might imagine, I don't often watch TV down in the den with my clothes off. Plus . . ." She stopped here.

"Plus what?"

"Something Dom left behind," Caitlin said, blushing. "On the sofa."

"A condom wrapper," Jennifer guessed.

"No, not that!" Caitlin said. "He left his underwear. Condoms. They're so gross, so embarrassing."

"But you *did* use one," Jennifer said. "I hate to sound like the Safe Sex Police, but with what's happening to Alan . . ."

"Jen, we did. And we will. Even though it seems a little ridiculous. I mean I can't imagine Dom has anything. He's from around here, he's Patti's brother, and besides, he's extremely clean."

"You mean, like, he takes showers?"

"Well, yeah," Caitlin said.

Jennifer got an exasperated look on her face. "You're supposed to be the brain of our class and you're telling me some guy you just went to bed with couldn't possibly have AIDS because he washes himself and because he's related to someone we know. Listen to yourself."

Caitlin felt chagrined. "I guess I'm not sounding too smart. It's just that it's so hard to deal with this issue. I mean, I didn't want to bring up the subject beforehand. That would've sounded like I already knew what was going to happen. Which I did, but still. And then when things started happening, the last thing I wanted to do was stop to have a big talk."

"I know it's hard," Jennifer said. "But it's important. To you and to me. I'm losing my boyfriend. I don't want my best friend putting herself at risk." She stopped a minute as they pushed through the revolving door into the mall. "The other day I had this thought," she went on when they were inside and walking side by side through the mall. "Like 'Boy, is it lucky Alan and I didn't ever sleep together.' And then I had this huge wave of guilt. Because, really, what I was saying to myself was 'You could've gotten it, and didn't.' "

"But what's wrong with that?" Caitlin asked.

"I don't know," Jennifer said. "It felt like I was betraying Alan. Being glad I'd never gotten close enough to a person I love to catch his suffering. It's almost as if I was saying I was glad it was him, and not me."

"Those kinds of thoughts are just natural," Caitlin said. "You can't help having them. Anyone would. You're being too hard on yourself. As for me, there might not *be* any more sex to be safe about. My parents have forbidden me to ever see him again. And . . ."

Jennifer put up a hand as they walked into The Gap. "*Please*. Don't even bother going on with whatever you were going to say. We both know you're going to see Dom again, somehow, on the sly, but for sure last night was not the end, only the beginning of a new phase. The Secret Phase. I love it. Caitlin Carney, River Bend's Good Girl of the Year, goes on the sly."

Jennifer was right. Even after Mr. Carney called Mr. Costa into his office for a chat about their children, Caitlin and Dom still managed to find ways to see each other. It just involved more deception. Which made them both feel bad but at the same time gave their romance an edge of excitement, of danger.

The old canoe camp was still a safe place. No one ever came there or knew that they did. On Dom's days off, they often met there for a few stolen hours. Today they had gone swimming and were drying off in the sun on the dock, alternately talking and kissing. Becoming lovers had banished the shyness they'd had with each other.

"I want to talk to you about something," he said to her, rolling onto his side as they lay together on a beach towel spread on the old dock.

She nodded for him to go ahead, having no idea what was on his mind.

"It's July," he said, "and soon it's going to be August. And then September. Are you still thinking of going away to Vassar?"

She was stunned. It was the first time either of them had mentioned the future.

"I don't know," she admitted. "My parents are being so hard on me since the night they caught us. They want me to go east early, to some optional orientation week. I just hate feeling so pressured by them. You know they never even asked me what college I wanted to go to. Since I could get in practically anywhere, they gave me a choice of five they thought were the best. Not the best for *me* necessarily. But the best in terms of prestige and status and chances of snagging a rich, successful, socially upscale husband."

"Like me," Dom said, brushing across her face the tip of a leaf he'd plucked.

"*Just* like you," Caitlin said, and she couldn't help smiling.

Dom then grew more serious. "What happens to us in September?"

"What do you think is going to happen?"

"That depends on you," he said. "If you go away, you know what'll happen. You'll say you'll write and I will, too, and we will, for a few letters, but then your letters will come less often, and they'll be filled

129

with a life you'll be leading without me. And then you'll come home at Christmas, and we'll be almost strangers, and you'll wonder what was so special about us this summer."

"Oh, Dom."

He put a finger to her lips. "You know what I'm saying is true."

"So what's the alternative?" she asked.

"You stay here, with me."

"And do what?"

"You could get a job. Be a secretary for someone. You got those great grades. Some business guy would be happy to have you."

"And you?"

"I like the job at the club. I like being out of doors, my own boss. You know. It's not much money, but we could live on it. My family manages somehow."

Caitlin shuddered inside at the thought of living a life like Dom and Patti's parents. Scrimping and saving and doing without and getting hand-me-down clothes from relatives for the little kids, and refinishing junk sale furniture for their house, and taking vacations with that awful old trailer hooked up behind their car. Surely he couldn't be imagining a life like that for them!

She didn't know what to say. She'd never felt like this about anyone before, but right now, this summer, she had Dom *plus* she still had her whole life here. Her friends and family. By fall, all the others except Patti would be going away, beginning the lives that lay beyond high school for them. Caitlin wanted to find out what was waiting for her out there in the wider world.

"You've already been everywhere," she told him. "You knew you wanted to come back because you'd already seen a lot else and made a decision. I haven't had that chance yet."

"It's different for girls," he said.

"Not for this girl," she said, suddenly wondering if — for all their supposed closeness — he even knew who she was.

Chapter 15

Having gone to bed at eight in the morning after getting home from work at the hospital, Jennifer was awakened a little before noon to the pulsating sounds of Scotty's bass-heavy boom box pumping rap music out of the room next to hers. She leapt out of bed and stormed in on him.

"You know those newspaper stories where the sweet sister — everyone loved her, she got good grades and was a cheerleader and all — suddenly goes berserk and murders her ten-year-old brother by throwing him and his tape deck out the window?"

"You are so uncool," Scotty said, reluctantly turning the music down.

"I am so exhausted, twerp," Jennifer said. "Wait until you get a summer job. Even if I'm in Hollywood directing movies by then, I'm going to put my career on hold for three months to come back to torment you."

"I love you, too," Scotty said to Jennifer's back as she was already headed fuzzily down the stairs (once she was up, she almost never could get back to sleep again) muttering, "Coffee. Coffee. My kingdom for a cup of coffee."

The day's mail was scattered across the front hall floor in front of the mail slot in the door. She went over and scooped it up on her way into the kitchen. Once she'd had half of her first cup of coffee and she was feeling alive if not exactly awake, she noticed that the fat envelope on the bottom of the pile was from UCLA and was addressed to her. She ripped it open and read the cover letter, which began:

"Dear Freshman," then went on to detail the orientation week set up in advance of the fall semester, a time for new students to get acquainted with the campus and dorms and cafeteria and college life in general. She read every word. She went over to the wall phone and dialed Caitlin's private, unlisted line. She wanted to make this all more real by telling it to her best friend.

"What're you up to?" she said when Caitlin answered.

"Oh, it's Patti's day off. She and I are going out to the flea market. Want to come?"

"No, I'm too exhausted to buy any fleas. I just wanted to read to you from my official orientation packet from UCLA. I'm now apparently a 'university woman.' When did we cross over that line — you know, from girl to woman?"

"For me it for sure happened this summer. For lots of reasons, but . . ."

". . . especially for one," Jennifer finished for her. "Yes, and we all know what that reason is."

"Ha ha," Caitlin said. "But really, it is kind of exciting to get all this mail treating you like an adult. I got a whole kit like that from Vassar. I can't believe how much stuff there is to do. You know, getting your roommate — mine's from Chicago — and your student number, and your class schedule. And your campus map. Yada yada. You know. I feel more like an astronaut being shot to the moon than just someone going to the next step in school."

"But that's just it," Jennifer said. "It's not just like going from junior to senior year. It's a total change in life-style. Dorms and cafeterias and no parents. No car because it's too far to bring it. I'm flying out with my bicycle, though. I've got to have some wheels. But basically, everything's going to be different. It's like taking our lives now, chopping them up in a million pieces, throwing them up in the air, and seeing where everything lands."

"I might not be going," Caitlin said.

"I think we might have a bad connection," Jennifer said. "I thought you just said you might not be going."

"I'm just *thinking* about it, is all."

"Like you want a *better* college than Vassar?" Jennifer said sarcastically.

"Like Vassar is probably fine, but it's the school my parents picked. I'm getting tired of living *their* version of my life. I'd like to start living my own version, only I'm not sure what that is."

"Does any of this by any chance have anything

to do with an extremely good-looking, grass-cutting guy?"

"Well, Dom does want me to stay here with him. So I guess that's a factor. But I don't know. I'm so in love with him, but I can't really see staying here. And I can't really ask him to come to college with me. He's not interested in higher education, and since he's already been everywhere, he's happy to finally be home. Just when I'm dying to get out. It's kind of bad timing, you might say."

"So what're you planning to do?" Jennifer asked, pulling a quart of milk out of the refrigerator and pouring some over the cereal she'd just shaken into a bowl.

"I don't know. I'm thinking. And I have to think fast. My parents would like to ship me out on the next plane. Get me out of harm's way. 'Harm' spelled with a capital D."

"Do they suspect? About you and Dom?"

"Oh, how can they not?" Caitlin said. "They haven't been able to catch me, but I'm sure they can see it all over my face. They're probably freaked out that I'm throwing myself away on what they consider some worthless bum. Which is the only way they can see him. But, hey, these are small potatoes compared to what you're going through. How's Alan doing?"

"Well, since he's been home, he's improved a lot, but he's not really up and around yet. He gets tired walking from his bedroom to the kitchen and back. I'm going over there now."

"Isn't it kind of early for you to be up?"

"Don't remind me," Jennifer said and groaned. "I am a victim of rap music."

Alan's parents both worked, and so he was home alone during the day. Jennifer came by when she woke up, usually in the early afternoon, and brought him news and gossip, books and videos, flowers and peanut butter cookies. Today she brought the packet from UCLA.

"What a dolt!" she said, knocking her forehead, as she noticed an identical envelope on the coffee table in front of the sofa Alan was stretched out on. "Of course you got one, too. Isn't it exciting?" She looked again. "But you haven't even opened yours."

"I guess I just haven't gotten around to it," he said, clicking the cable remote to a show teaching Japanese. He was still in his pajama bottoms. There was an egg muffin sandwich his mother had probably microwaved and set out for him, but it was untouched and cold on the coffee table. Even though his parents and Jennifer were after him all the time to eat, he seemed to have lost his appetite and was getting thinner, even though the pneumonia was gone.

"Well, I can see why," Jennifer said sarcastically about his not bothering with the UCLA packet. "With your busy schedule and all. I mean, it's only about our immediate future."

"*Your* immediate future, you mean."

She looked at him, bewildered.

"Well," he said. "Do I *look* like someone who's about to dash off to college?" She looked at his pale complexion, his concave chest under his T-shirt with the ribs bowed out beneath it, his hair matted to the back of his head like her hospital patients. She had to admit Alan didn't look up to a walk around the block, let alone to going off to college in California.

"But we don't have to go until September. You've got plenty of time to spring back. Are you drinking your carrot juice?" She had just noticed the undrunk glass of it next to the sandwich. "Come on. Are you going to help yourself along, or just sink into despair?"

"I thought I'd sink into despair," he said. "You have any better ideas?" He had never been like this — sarcastic and negative — when he was well. It was as though just managing his physical problems and limitations took everything out of him, and he had nothing left over for good humor or optimism. More than anything else, hope was what Jennifer tried to give him, but it was hard when he was in this kind of brick-wall mood.

"You're feeling better. We've got you practically a room full of vitamins and every article Leah's mom could come up with. You're on the most up-to-the-minute medications available. You know people are living longer and longer with the virus. I think you've got to look at the pneumonia as a setback you've gotten beyond. And I think part of living is acting on the assumption that you are going to continue to live. What other option do you have?"

"Admitting I'm probably not going to California with you."

Jennifer sat down next to him on the couch, took the remote out of his hand and clicked the TV off. "Look, this isn't an either/or proposition. We either go together, or neither of us goes."

"Don't be ridiculous," he said, ruffling her hair. "If I'm not up to going in September, you go on ahead of me and I'll try to catch up with you in January. You can be my advance scouting party. See if California is too laid-back for a go-getter like me."

She put her head on his chest, and he held her for a long time while neither of them said anything. She felt torn. She didn't want to leave him, but he was probably right that there was no point in both of them staying here. He could start midyear, but if she didn't take her scholarship in September, they'd award it to one of the runners-up.

"We don't have to decide any of this right now," she said, ducking the whole issue.

"Right," he said, and she could tell from his tone that she had failed the pop quiz. She was supposed to say of course she wouldn't think of leaving him, not for anything. There were moments — and this was one of them — when, in spite of knowing it was selfish and unreasonable, she resented Alan for taking away the easy, happy life she'd be living now if she wasn't tied to him. And then, of course, she pulled back and looked at him and felt horrible for even allowing herself this thought.

"Caitlin! Slow down, you maniac!" Patti shouted over the wind and the racing engine of the Miata.

"You are such a granny," Caitlin said, lifting her foot off the accelerator.

"Look! There's a sign for it," Patti said, pointing to a rickety homemade billboard.

ROLLINS COUNTY FLEA MARKET
SAT, SUN, DAWN TO DUSK
5 MI AHEAD ON COUNTY RD 12

It was Sunday, Patti's day off, and she and Caitlin had decided to go see this flea market, which was getting famous around their part of Texas. When they got there, they found a parking lot with a thousand cars and rows and rows of booths selling everything imaginable. Quilts and chests and old records and toys outgrown long ago by children who were probably old and gray by now. They walked for what seemed like many miles and several hours. Patti wound up buying a bedspread embroidered with a giant ear of corn. "I love stuff that's corny," she said with a sly grin.

"Ow," Caitlin said, letting Patti know the pun had hurt her ears.

"I refuse to be made fun of by someone who bought this stupid ventriloquist's dummy," Patti countered, as they headed for one of the refreshment wagons.

"I might well need it for a new career," Caitlin said, "that is, if I don't go off to college."

This stopped Patti in her tracks.

"What?! You not going to college? *You*, Miss Collegiate. And with money in the bank for it. Why wouldn't you? I mean, what would you do instead?"

"I don't know. I might just stay here. Keep you company after the others all leave in the fall."

Patti gave Caitlin the fishy eye. "I don't think I'm the Costa you'd be staying for. Am I right?"

Caitlin didn't want to talk about something she was still so unsure of herself, and so she was evasive with Patti. She stepped up to the window of the refreshment wagon and ordered hot dogs and sodas for both of them.

"Well, tell me," Patti said as they carried their food to one of the tables set up in a field beyond the wagons. "Are you thinking of staying around this nowhere town on account of my brother?"

"Maybe."

Patti turned to her friend and looked her hard in the eyes. "I can't believe you're thinking of just throwing away something I'd die to have."

"Like what?"

"Like a chance to get out of this dry gulch of a town. Go to college. Meet new people. Be away from my family. Not that I don't love them like crazy, but being the big sister has always made me sort of a junior mom all these years. I don't even know who I am. Who I'd be if I didn't have the little ones hanging on me, my mother counting on me."

"Then why don't you just go?"

"Caitlin. Get a grip. Where would the money come from?"

"Well, your parents. Surely they must have put something away for your education."

"They haven't put enough away for next week's

groceries. Not everybody's father owns an oil company."

"Why are you sniping at me?" Caitlin said, wounded.

"I'm just asking you to take off your rose-colored glasses and see what the hard realities are for other people. For me."

"So it's not just your indecision that's been holding you back from college?"

Patti shook her head. "It's what I want more than anything else. So you can see why I'm freaked to hear you'd give it all up for someone else. Especially for Dom!"

"Patti! What a way to talk about your own brother."

"It's not Dom. It's you and Dom. I love you both, but you are polar opposites. You're intellectual; he's physical. You're together; he's a space cadet."

"Patti!"

"It's true. Dad had to drive over to the club last night with a locksmith. Dom says his keys to the pickup were stolen, but give me a break. You know he just left them somewhere and can't admit he's just totally absent-minded."

"If we're so opposite," Caitlin challenged, "then how come we're so much in love?"

"Because opposites attracts. Everyone knows that." Patti had a million sayings like this that she repeated as though they had to be true if people had been saying them for so long. "But birds of a feather flock together. Which means that you're attracted to Dom now because he's different, but when it comes down to living your whole life, you've got to get someone whose ideas run alongside your own. Even though he's a dyed-in-the-wool American, I think there are some Italian male genes deep down inside Dom. He wants a wife who'll be in the kitchen stirring the kettle, minding the bambinos."

"Come on," Caitlin said after swallowing a bite of hot dog. "You're kidding."

"You mean you've never talked about any of this?" Patti shook her head. "You two really ought to come up for air sometime and compare notes on who you are. I'm telling you, Dom does not want a wife with a college degree and some career of her own. He wants a marriage like my parents. Lots of kids, lots of home life, and him at the head of the table."

Caitlin started laughing.

"You think I'm kidding, don't you?" Patti said. "Well, why don't you ask the man himself? It sounds like you're going to be quite surprised by what you hear."

"Okay," Caitlin said, taking up the challenge. "I'll ask him. And then I'll tell you how wrong you are."

"I'm not wrong," Patti said, shaking her head. "You'll see."

Chapter 16

"Tomatoes, thirty-six cans," Danny called down from the top of the ladder. Patti, sitting on a huge stack of rice, took this down on an inventory sheet. The two of them were in the large storeroom at the back of the grill's kitchen, taking stock. "Corn, twenty large cans. Better mark that for a reorder," he said as he headed down the ladder.

"That all?" Patti asked, getting up off the rice sack.

"Yeah, but can you stay a minute? There's something I need to talk to someone about, and you might as well be the someone."

"Well, when you put it in such flattering terms, how can I refuse?"

"I'm sorry," Danny said, putting his arm around Patti. "What I meant was I'm bursting at the seams with this, and you're the most understanding person I know, *and* one of my closest friends, and so I've decided you're the best person to come to with this."

"So, shoot. I'm all ears."

"Well, the thing is I'm pretty hopelessly in love with Leah."

"Leah who?"

"Leah, who?! Leah Shore. Leah, our old and dear rain dancer friend!" Danny said, incredulous. "What other Leah *is* there?"

"But Leah?! You two have known each other a hundred years. Even before the rain dancers. Didn't she dump a pail of sand on your head, or something, when you were little?"

"It was mud," Danny said.

"Right. And I can remember her hitting you with the cast on her arm after she broke it on the playground. And then there was the time her mother fixed us that weird curry dinner, and you threw up for hours in her bathroom. And then there was her bee sting. What I mean is how can you all of a sudden have romantic feelings for someone you've seen all swollen up like a melon?"

"I knew you'd be understanding and sympathetic," Danny said.

Patti laughed. "I'm sorry. It's just so hard to imagine. Does she know?"

"No. She's probably like you. She probably couldn't imagine it."

"How long have you been feeling this way?"

"I don't know. Since last year anyway. Boy, you sound like a doctor asking me how long I've noticed these symptoms," Danny said, and Patti kiddingly pressed her palm to his forehead.

"Patient seems to have a serious case," she said. "Drastic measures will be required."

"Like what?"

"Well, I think you ought to let her know."

"I tried the other night when we went to the show, but all I was doing was irritating her by blocking her view of Greg Wright."

"Yeah, she definitely has a megacrush on him. That'll pass, though."

"You think?"

"Sure. She's just a little nutty on the subject; she's not a lunatic. A little while longer of getting no response from him, and she'll give up the ghost."

"But I don't have much time to wait. I've got to make my move before we're packing up to go to school in different parts of the country."

"Don't panic. It's still only July. You've got time. Just chill out for a while, and I'll put a bug in her ear."

"Oh, no!" he moaned. "That might be even worse."

"Trust me," Patti said, pulling at the tip of his shirt collar. "I'm incredibly subtle. I'm just going to plant the idea in her head."

"I think what I need is voodoo. You know, where we'd put a love potion in her food, and suddenly she'd fall in love with me without even knowing why."

The two of them walked out of the storeroom and into the kitchen. Brice was there, sweating profusely from being out on the course, looking extra goony in yellow bermudas with his green and red bowling shoes. He was getting himself a Coke from the soda machine. Danny and Patti nodded hi and shifted their conversation into code, so he wouldn't know what was going on. The less Brice knew about anything, the better, as far as they were concerned.

"Well, I'm off now," Patti said, punching her time card in the machine by the employees' entrance. "Think I'll stop by the library."

"Thanks, Patti," Danny said as she walked out the door. He turned back and headed for the phone to call suppliers and place orders for the kitchen's storeroom. Brice just stood there drinking his Coke, not making a move to leave. Danny looked up from his notes to find Brice staring at him.

"Something I can do for you, Fraser?" he said, last-naming him as though he were an underling, which, at least among club staff, he was.

"Tyler called me into his office this morning to find out what I knew about the thefts around here." Danny had heard indirectly, through his father, that these were still going on, with increasingly large amounts being lifted out of the wallets of members.

"So, I gather he suspected you right off the bat," Danny said, needling Brice.

"No, you little moron. He wanted my opinion on who I thought was doing it."

"I can't wait to hear what you told him," Danny said.

Brice looked around and over Danny's head as if he were too bored to continue the conversation, but would force himself to talk with someone so far beneath him. "I told him my suspicions led me to Dom Costa."

"But why would Dom do something like that?"

146

"Well, because he must be especially feeling his lack of funds now that he, as I've heard, is seeing quite a bit of our town's little rich girl, Caitlin Carney. Myself, I think she could do a lot better than that hood. Someone in her own social class, for instance. And perhaps with Mr. Costa out of the way, she'll be able to see that more clearly."

"By someone in her social class," Danny said, "I assume you mean yourself."

"Maybe," Brice said, acting mysterious. "But I've told you enough for today."

And with that, he tossed his cup of Coke into the garbage bin. It was nearly full and splashed all over.

Brice turned at the door and noticed this. "You'll probably want to wipe that mess up, Sanchez, being in charge of the kitchen and all," he said as the screen door slammed behind him.

Patti called Danny that night and told him, "I talked with Leah."

"Yeah. And?"

"Well, I didn't get to the part about you."

"What do you mean you didn't get to that part? That's the *only* part."

"No, first there's the part about her and Greg. She wouldn't let me get a word in edgewise between her stream of gaga-ness about him. Did you know that Greg's favorite color is blue, and he likes his hamburgers *without* mustard?"

"But there *is* no her and Greg. It's all just a big fantasy," Danny said.

"You know that. I know that. Greg knows that.

Leah's just the last to know. But eventually she'll figure it out."

"And then she'll come rushing into my arms?"

"Well," Patti said, now having to shout over the screams of her little brothers and sister. Phone conversations between their houses, both packed with big families, were just about impossible. "At least then you'll have a fighting chance," Patti went on. "Which you don't right now, I'm telling you — not as long as she's blinded by her crush."

Danny didn't say anything.

"Hey," Patti said in response to his silence, "I went through something like this last year. Remember? I was so wrecked over Wynn Clark. He didn't know I existed on the planet."

"But how did that turn out?"

"He never did find out I live on the planet."

"Thanks, Patti. You've been a big help. Now if you'll excuse me while I go cry myself to sleep."

"But the point is I got over him," she said.

"And my point is, I don't *want* to get over Leah."

"Well, maybe something will happen. Something that'll make her see you in a new light."

And something did. It just took another week or so.

August

Chapter 17

It was Sunday, and Leah was over at the club pool, swimming and trying ever so subtly (and oh so unsuccessfully) to get Greg's attention. Then, for a while, she was hanging out behind the kitchen door, chatting with Danny before the dinner crowd came in. Greg was just getting off and had changed from his swim trunks into black leather motorcycle jeans and a red T-shirt.

"Doesn't he look fabulous?" Leah asked Danny.

"Yeah, none of us can get a thing done around here," Danny said. "We're all too busy watching Greg and thinking how fabulous he is."

Leah took a swing and fake-punched him in the arm. "Come on. You're supposed to be my friend. You should be supporting me in this."

"I can't, Leah. I just don't think it's something that's going to happen. Greg already has a girl-friend, with whom he seems perfectly happy. When guys are happy with their girlfriends, they don't usually go looking for other girls. And if they do, then they're not the kind of guys I want my, my, uh, friends to be throwing themselves at."

Leah flushed and grew suddenly fierce. "I am not *throwing myself* at anyone," she said and stomped out of the kitchen and into the parking lot, where she was just able to catch up with Greg.

"Hey, uh, Greg!" she said, trying to sound normal, but it came out as a shout.

He turned around.

"Hey, Linda, how's it going?" he said.

"Well, it's Leah actually. Remember?" she said.

"Right," he said, then stood there waiting for her to say something.

"I saw you heading toward your motorcycle and I was just on my way home and I know you live near there" — immediately she wondered, *Why did I say that? Argh. I sound like one of those creeps who follow movie stars around* — "and well, I was just wondering if you could give me a lift?"

"Oh. Sure. Get on," he said as he straddled the bike and flipped down the foot rests over the back wheel. As she got on behind him, he handed her his helmet. "I've only got one," he told her.

It was wonderful. The inside smelled like his hair.

When he had kick-started the bike and revved it a few times with the hand throttle, Leah got on and put her arms around him from behind. She could feel the warmth of his back beneath his shirt. This was exactly how she imagined being with Greg, and she pushed the fantasy ahead, to the part where they were racing against the wind on his motorcycle.

She wanted to press her cheek against his back, but the helmet got in the way.

"Hey!" he shouted back over his shoulder. "What're you trying to do — knock me out?"

It was about then that the two other guys who lifeguarded at the pool — Ray Crawford and Joel Feldman — came out into the parking lot.

"Hey, Wright!" Ken called. "Do a wheelie for us!"

"Yeah, Evel Kneivel!" Joel egged Greg on.

Greg laughed and shouted back to them, "I've never tried it with somebody on back, but what the heck."

Before Leah had a chance to object, she felt the motorcycle's engine roaring beneath her. Suddenly the bike hit a patch of oil on the asphalt, and she was detached from the bike and Greg, suspended, free, until gravity kicked in and brought her to the ground.

The next thing she knew, Greg had wheeled around and was looking down at her. She could see the other two guys disappearing around the side of the clubhouse — not wanting any connection with the mishap, she figured.

"Sorry about that. You all right?" Greg asked her.

Leah nodded and sat up. She had bloody scrapes on both elbows and knees, but she could move everything so she didn't think anything was broken.

And then Danny was rushing across the parking lot toward her. "I heard something and came out to see — " he said, dropping to his knees. "Are you okay?"

She could see real concern in his eyes, instead of the polite minimum interest in Greg's as he said, "Hey, Dan, as long as nothing major's wrong, and you're here to take care of her, I'm going to take off. I'm supposed to pick up Shannon in half an hour, and I've got to go home and change first."

Leah knew a more pressing reason was he didn't want Ken Tyler to come out and find him in the middle of this scene. Tyler was death on employees fooling around on club premises. Greg pulled the bike around and looked down at Leah.

Maybe he's finally seeing me, seeing me as someone special, Leah thought.

"Yes?" she said tentatively.

"Uh, well, could I have my helmet back?"

When he'd roared off, Danny asked Leah, "Do you think you can stand up?"

She nodded, only half hearing him through her rage at Greg and her embarrassment at her own foolishness for ever thinking he cared a bit about her. She moved to get back on her feet while Danny put her arm over his shoulder and lifted her.

"I think you look worse than you really are," he said. "I've got a first-aid kit inside. The box of a thousand Band-Aids."

When they were in the kitchen, Danny sat her down on a high stool. He got a wet towel and began cleaning her scrapes.

"Ouch!" Leah shouted and pulled her elbow away.

"Want me to get you a bullet to bite on?"

"No," she said, smiling. "I can take it."

"I'm an expert at scrapes," he said. "Comes with being a big brother."

"I feel like such an idiot," she said as he taped a giant Band-Aid over her elbow.

"Why? You didn't do anything stupid. You were just an innocent passenger. Greg's the idiot. Trying to do a wheelie with someone on the back of the bike."

"But I shouldn't have been there," Leah said. "That's the stupid part. That I've wasted half the school year and now half the summer trying to get his attention, when the truth is I'm practically invisible to him. He couldn't care less about me. This just proves it. How did I not see it before, though?"

"You didn't want to, that's why."

"How could I have been so blind?"

"Not blind," Danny said, dabbing Mercurochrome on her knee. "Just nearsighted. You were looking so closely at Greg, you couldn't see that someone else was standing a little farther off, caring about you, wanting you. Loving you."

"Who?" Leah said. She couldn't imagine who he was talking about.

"Me," he said and dropped his gaze to the floor, not able to meet her eyes.

"Oh, Danny. That's what those odd looks were the night we sat up at the hospital. That's why you wanted me to stop ogling Greg in the show. Now everything's falling into place."

"You make it sound like just a detective story. Like it's all over now that you've figured out the clues. You haven't told me what you think about it."

"Well," Leah said, laughing a little. "You have to admit, it's pretty surprising. I mean, you've had quite a bit of time to think about this, and I've had about five seconds."

"But you think there's a chance? A possibility?"

Leah looked at him intently, a rush of thoughts going through her head, not all of them making sense. Finally, she said, "Yes, I think there might be a possibility."

Because she was looking at him so intently, their faces were quite close, and it was easy for him to lean a little more toward her and kiss her. It was a very soft kiss, really several little kisses, all fluttery and sweet.

"I'm going to need something more substantial to base my decision on," she teased him, and their mouths met again, but in a different way.

"I'll have those great sour cream and guacamole chicken things you fix," Mr. Carney said to Raul Sanchez, Danny's father. The Carneys were having dinner at Playa del Sol, the fancy restaurant run by the Sanchez family.

"Señor Carney will have the enchiladas suizas," Mr. Carney told the waiter.

Caitlin's father smiled. He enjoyed being treated like a big shot, which he was in this restaurant, in River Bend, all across the southern part of the state. Oil was money and money — as the saying went — talked. When Frank Carney talked, people listened. He was not a man used to being contradicted. And so he was quite stunned when, a little ways into their dinner, his daughter did just that. The matter under discussion was Caitlin going east early next month, taking a few days in New York City, then going up to the optional orientation week at Vassar. What was going unspoken in all the talk at the table was the true purpose of this early departure — namely, to put as much distance as possible, as soon as possible, between her and Dom. Her parents couldn't be sure Caitlin was still seeing him, but she knew they suspected. They weren't dumb.

"Your mother and I thought it might be fun if all of us went together. Made a family trip of it. We could go to New York, stay at the Plaza, eat at some fancy restaurants, go to the top of the Empire State Building. You know, just be tourists. Then we could tag along with you for the first days of this orientation thing. The folder said parents are welcome."

"Dad," Caitlin said, trying to think how to word this without getting him crazy. "I don't think that would be the best thing."

Mr. Carney immediately stopped eating. He stopped with his fork, heavy with refried beans, in midair. "What do you mean, not the best thing?" he said, but it wasn't really a question.

"Well, it's just that I've been doing a lot of thinking this summer," she said. "And, well, the thing is, I'm not all that sure that college is the best idea for me right now. I mean, I've been going to school since I was five. I might like to take a break for a year. They allow delayed enrollment for a year after you've been accepted. I called."

"You *called*?!" her father said, his normally pink face going dark red. "Who gave you permission to call?"

"You didn't mention any calling to *me*, dear," her mother said.

This was going to be horrible, Caitlin could see. Truly horrible. But she had to hang tough.

"Look," she said. "You want me to go to college, and I'm pretty sure I want to, too. This just might not be the right time."

"And what would you do instead?" her mother asked.

"I know what she'd do," Caitlin's father said. "She'd hang out around here with that piece of trash lawn mower. I won't have it. I'll run that kid back out of town and onto some ship that's going to be out to sea for a couple of years." He glared at Caitlin. "And don't think I won't do it."

"Dad. This isn't about Dom." (Well, that was partly true. It wasn't *all* about Dom.) "This is about me. I'm capable of thinking for myself. And now that I'm doing just that, you're screaming and threatening me. Well, I won't have *that*," she said as she got up, dropped her napkin on her chair, and headed out of the restaurant.

"Was there something wrong with your dinner?" Danny's father asked her when she got to the door.

"It wasn't the food, Mr. Sanchez. It was the company."

158

She walked out of the air-conditioning, into the hot night.

She thought she'd head over to Ernie's Shell Station, where she had a pretty good idea she'd find Dom.

Chapter 18

"Go get some lunch, honey," Leah's mother said to her when they were done reshelving the day's returned books. Leah enjoyed working in the library way more than she'd thought she would. She liked answering questions and helping people find out stuff. She especially liked working with the little kids who came in and tottered out under mile-high stacks of books they could barely carry home.

She'd been distracted the past couple of weeks, though. Ever since Danny had told her how he felt about her. Her first reaction had been that it was a little silly, two such old friends falling in love. But Danny clearly *had* fallen in love with her, and every time she thought of him putting those Band-Aids on her knees and elbows, her eyes welled up with tears over how sweet and caring he'd been when she really needed him. As opposed to Greg Wright, who'd peeled off on his motorcycle.

And then there was the way Danny kissed. He always seemed such a character and such a high-energy friend, she wouldn't have been able to imagine him calming down enough to be tender. But she was wrong! Even those first kisses in the grill's kitchen — not the most romantic setting in the world — had been great.

She'd told him this at the time, and he'd said, "Well, I've been saving them up for quite a while."

Since then, they'd done quite a bit of kissing (and a little more), and it was all great. Still, she wasn't sure she could fall in love with him. She'd mentioned this to Patti, who told her, "You don't have to make up your mind this week. There's no deadline. You can just take your time and see what happens, see how you feel as you go along."

Which was exactly what she'd been doing. It was different. Before, she'd had all these fantasies about Greg, but no reality. With Danny, most of the romance was happening for real. And so she didn't fantasize so much. Which left her with lots more time to just be in her life, living it, not making up how she'd like it to be. It was different and felt good.

"Do you want me to pick up something for you?" she asked her mother, who often had her lunch in her office at the back of the library. "I could stop at Wong's and get some fried rice."

"Why don't you just get us a couple of sandwiches over at the 7-Eleven?" she said. "And an iced tea for me."

"Will do," Leah said, heading for the front door.

The 7-Eleven was just a block away, away from the center of town, toward the highway. Lots of

Rio Rojo kids used the parking lot as a hangout. There were a couple of guys — next year's seniors — standing at the pay phone when she walked up. They nodded at her.

She went into the store and told Andy, the day manager, "Two egg salad sandwiches when you have a minute."

He nodded and finished checking out a customer. Leah headed toward the back of the store, where the soda cooler was. She just wanted a Coke, which was easy. There were about a hundred cans in the little slots behind the glass of the cooler cabinets. Her mother, though, liked iced tea that came in cans and it wasn't always so easy to find. Leah had to bend way over and look into the bottom slots of the cooler in the farthest corner of the store. Which is where she was when she heard someone shout, "All right, everybody! On the floor, hands above your heads! You too, goonface!"

Leah realized in an instant that the store was being held up!

She did exactly as the voice said. She got face-down on the floor and stretched her hands out in front of herself. The robber kept talking the whole time, in a fake calm voice. First to the customers in the store.

"All right, I want you all to line up against the magazine rack over there. Put your hands behind your backs where I can see them."

Something about his voice was familiar, but Leah couldn't place it. She was just about to get up and join the others when she heard him say, "Okay.

That's good. Now you all just stay calm and don't make any heroic moves."

From the way he was talking, she could tell he thought he had everybody in his little lineup. Because she'd been bent over behind all the aisles, he hadn't seen her! If she just kept still, he wouldn't know she was there.

She could see *him*, though, through the wire mesh of a rack holding chips and cheese curls. Really, what she could see was his shoes. They were peculiar. Somehow familiar, like the voice.

Now he was ordering Andy around.

"Okay, dumbbell, take all the cash out of that register and put it in a paper bag. No stupid moves. No pressing any alarm buttons. I'll see it if you do, and I'll be forced to use this."

He had a gun. Knowing this all of a sudden made Leah realize this wasn't a game of hide and seek, that this guy would probably kill her if he saw her moving. She started shaking in spite of knowing it was the absolute worst thing she could do. She could hear the bags of chips above her rattling from the vibrations of her shuddering body against the rack. She inched away from it and hoped he hadn't noticed.

Although the robbery probably took all of five minutes, the time passed like hours. She thought Andy would never get all that money into the bag. But finally he must have, because the holdup guy said, "All right, stupido, down on the floor like everybody else. I'm going to back out. I'll be able to see all of you until I get in my truck. So nobody moves unless you want to make the ten o'clock news — as the body they're wheeling out of here."

And then he was gone. Leah stayed on the floor for a long time. Even though she could hear the others getting up and beginning to talk about the robbery. Finally, while Andy was on the phone calling the police, she got up, smoothed her skirt, and brushed a streak of dirt off her blouse. By then everyone else in the store was buzzing about the robbery, and how close they'd come to getting shot, and how brave they'd been. What had the robber looked like? Their descriptions didn't seem to match. Some people thought he was tall; others said he had a medium build.

When the police came, they asked all of them if they were all right and what they'd seen so they could put together a description. Leah didn't figure that, having been the furthest away and down on the floor, she'd have anything to add. And it looked like the police were going to take forever, writing down everything each customer and Andy had told them. She knew her mother was expecting her back by now, plus she just wanted to get out of the store and calm down. So she just walked out the front door. No one noticed her.

She was still pretty shook up when she got to the library and told the whole story to her mother, who immediately hugged her.

"Oh, honey! To think you were in so much danger!"

"I'm okay now," Leah said, trying to sound brave, although she was secretly happy her mother was coddling her a little. At the moment, she really needed it.

"Are you sure you shouldn't give your statement to the police?" her mother said. "I mean maybe you have a clue that would help them and don't know it."

"I don't think so, Mom. Everybody else saw a lot more than I did. They know it was either a medium-sized guy or a tall one and that he was driving a black pickup truck. Nobody saw his face or hair because he was wearing a ski mask."

"It's just so awful thinking of you in a situation like that," her mother said. "I can't believe this sort of thing can happen here in River Bend, where people have always trusted each other and don't have to worry about locking their doors at night. It's hard to imagine anyone around here doing something like this." She sighed. "I suppose it must've been someone who needs money."

Something about her mother's hypothetical description and the black pickup truck suddenly gelled in her mind into one terrible thought. What if the holdup guy was Dom?

The next day after work, she was over at the club playing tennis with Caitlin. She hadn't said anything to her about the possibility that Dom was the robber. She stuck to her story about not really seeing whoever did it, and how scared she'd been, and how she was just glad to have gotten out of the situation alive.

And then something came along to jog Leah's

memory, to make her realize she *had* seen something particular and peculiar about the gunman. This happened while Caitlin was off the court, fetching a ball that Leah had lobbed over the fence, when a foursome of women golfers came back to the clubhouse in two carts. As they were heading toward the clubhouse with their caddies behind them, Leah looked over. One of the golfers was Cheryl Lang, her mother's best friend. She waved at her, and only then did she notice that Cheryl's caddy was Brice. And only then did she notice his shoes. She was about the same distance (maybe a little further off) as she had been in the 7-Eleven. They were the same shoes. She'd thought they looked familiar during the robbery, but they were so out of context there. They were Brice's stupid red and green golf shoes! Brice was the guy who'd held up the 7-Eleven. (And gotten away with almost $2,000, according to the *River Bend Times* that morning.)

What should she do? Call the police? Confront Brice and give him a chance to defend himself? She didn't know, and so she just stood there.

"Are you still playing?" she heard Caitlin shout from across the court. "Or have you drifted off for the day?" Her friends were always teasing her for being spacey, but this time she had good reason.

She caught up with Brice behind the men's locker room. He was taking bags of clubs off the electric carts and putting them into the storage area.

"Brice," Leah said, "there's something we need to talk about."

"Yeah?" he said, not bothering to look at her. "And what could that possibly be?"

"I saw your shoes yesterday," she began haltingly. "In the 7-Eleven. During the holdup."

He turned sharply and glared at her. "But you weren't there . . ." He stopped and realized that he'd just given himself away and switched gears completely. "I mean, what are you talking about? What 7-Eleven? I don't have the vaguest idea what you're talking about."

"You do," Leah said. She wasn't going to let a goon like Brice Fraser intimidate her. "You know *exactly* what I'm talking about."

"Oh, yes," Brice said slowly, looking off into the distance as though he were an amnesia victim just getting his memory back. "I did hear something on the news about that robbery. I believe they already have a suspect in the matter. Our greenskeeper, Dom Costa. Apparently he dropped his keys in the parking lot on the way in. I guess he must have had a spare set to get away. But the police matched up the set in the lot to his truck. They were looking for a black pickup, and so it didn't require much heavy detective work on their part. Your friend Caitlin will be upset, I'm sure. For a little while anyway."

"Look, Brice," Leah said, now angry. "I don't know what kind of dirty tricks you're playing. Or why you're playing them on Dom. But you know and I know it was you who held up that store, and the only reason I'm talking to you about it is to give you a chance to turn yourself in. Maybe they'll go easier on you that way."

Brice laughed a sickening laugh, a slimy chuckle.

"Thank you so much, Leah, for thinking of me. Now run along and play your little games with your little friends. Maybe your mother will buy you a junior detective kit and you can take fingerprints and look at them with a magnifying glass. Maybe she can get you a Clue game and you can find out it was done by Colonel Mustard with the rope in the billiard room."

By this time, Leah was so mad she just said, "Sorry for bothering you, Brice. I didn't want to take this to the police, but now I will," and she stalked off to find a phone and call Danny.

"Just tell him what you know," Danny said when they were inside River Bend Police Station, sitting across an old wooden desk from a uniformed cop whose nameplate said he was Sergeant Becker. He'd been on the phone for quite some time. Finally he hung up.

"What can I do for you?"

"I think I have information that might help in that 7-Eleven robbery yesterday. I was there and . . ."

"Oh," he said. "One of the witnesses. Let's see if I can find your statement. What's your name?" He pulled out a list as he was speaking.

"Uh, well, I don't think I'm on your list. I didn't give any statement to the police who showed up. I didn't think I really had anything valuable to say. Now, though, I do."

"Wait a minute," the desk sergeant said, putting

his list down. "You were there — or at least you *say* you were there — but you never gave the police your name. Now you're coming forward with information?"

"Yes, I know who did it," she said. "I know who the robber was."

"Well, Miss, so do we. Or at least we've got a lot of evidence pointing to a particular party. We arrested him this morning."

"But you've got the wrong person!" Leah practically screamed. "Dom didn't do it."

The sergeant was not impressed. He droned on in a monotone. "The keys to his truck, which was noted by several passersby as being parked in front of the store at the time of the crime, were found in the parking lot. I believe his family is trying to make bail for him, but for the time being, at any rate, he's safely in the back" — he nodded over his shoulder — "under lock and key."

"No!" Leah pleaded. "You have to let him out. You have the wrong person. I saw the robber's shoes. It was Brice Fraser."

The sergeant began to laugh. "Oh, that's a good one," he said. "The richest man in the county robbing a 7-Eleven!"

"Not him. His *son*," Danny said, trying to sound calm and reasonable. "He wears these two-toned bowling shoes and those were the shoes Leah saw on the robber."

The sergeant smiled and said, "We can't really arrest someone on the basis of his shoes, even when reported by a sterling witness like yourself" — he gestured toward Leah — "whom no one saw, and who couldn't bother to make a report until now. Are you sure you kids aren't playing games with me? Maybe setting up a friend you don't like so much?"

"No way!" Danny said.

"Giving false evidence is a crime, you know," Sergeant Becker said.

"What we're telling you is the *truth*!" Leah shouted.

"If you'll excuse me," the sergeant said, putting the papers back into their folder. "I have to go back to the dull world of real police work. Where boring facts count more than exciting fiction."

"I can't believe he wouldn't even listen to us," Leah said when they'd come out of the police station. "And that Dom's in jail for something he didn't do. Caitlin must be frantic."

"She probably doesn't know yet. How would she have found out?"

"Well, if she has, her parents are probably delighted. She can't very well run off with a guy who's behind bars," Danny said. "I wonder why Brice is trying to pin this on Dom, though. He hardly knows the guy."

"This morning when he practically blurted out the truth to me, he let something about Caitlin slip. I think maybe he's still carrying a torch for her, and with his twisted reasoning, he might think that with Dom out of the way, he'll actually have a chance with her."

Danny looked thoughtful for a moment, then said, "I think we've got to get all the rain dancers together and brainstorm. We've got to find a way to get Dom out of trouble and Brice in. Where he belongs."

Chapter 19

Jennifer pulled her white nurse shoes off with her toes. She was too exhausted to untie them. She was also too exhausted even to sit up while waiting for the coffee maker to finish dripping and was lying flat on her back on the bench of the breakfast nook table.

"I guess I won't ask if it was a rough shift. You look like a beleaguered, weary intern, not a nurse's aide," her father said; coming into the kitchen to grab some coffee himself. "And you certainly don't look like an aspiring filmmaker. In fact I don't think I've seen you out with the videocam all summer."

"It hasn't turned out to be the kind of summer you want to capture in film highlights, if you know what I mean," she said.

"You mean Alan," her father said.

"He's not springing back," Jennifer said. "I tell everybody he is, but he isn't."

"I know," Dr. Novak said.

"How long do you think he has?" Jennifer asked,

sitting up and taking the mug of coffee her dad handed her.

In answer to her question, he shrugged. "It's hard to tell with AIDS. Sometimes, just when we think we've lost someone, they pop back and return to work or school for months, a year. Sometimes they're dead within a week of being diagnosed. Alan seems to be losing ground, but he could hang in there for a while."

"But probably not."

"But probably not," her father conceded. "You know, one thing you couldn't catch on tape is how much you've grown this summer. How you've really become an adult. Lots of girls would've crumbled, but you didn't. You're as strong as I've ever seen a support person be. You're probably the single most important factor in Alan's being as back on his feet as he is."

"I am?"

"The human spirit — the will to live or whatever you want to call it — is always the X-factor in any patient's survival. We can give Alan medication, but you're the one who's made him want to stick around, even though he's sick and tired of being sick."

"I never thought about it that way," Jennifer admitted.

"That's because you haven't thought about anything except Alan in the past couple of months. And you need to. Which brings me to my incredibly great idea."

"If you're going to offer to make me your horrible, rubbery fried eggs . . ." Jennifer said, holding up a hand to stop this possibility.

Her dad in turn put up *his* hand. "Please. I'm proposing much more than eggs. I'm wondering if you'll come up to Dallas with me over the weekend. I've got that cardiology conference, and your mother's on call in Maternity both days. I could use my clout to get you off work. You could do a little museum hopping, a little shopping while I'm busy, and then I promise to take you out for great dinners. We can stay with Aunt Dorothy and Uncle Bill. You know. A Jennifer Special weekend. Since I just took Scotty white-water rafting, I don't think he'll put up too much of a fuss about you getting your turn to do something fun."

Jennifer almost started crying. "I'd forgotten about Jennifer Specials."

These were an old-time thing her father used to do for her when she was little. They included going to the park and staying on the swings as long as she wanted; having fried shrimp at Benny's, a drive-in outside town; and riding a pony at Spenglers' Corral. These outings had sort of gotten dropped as Jennifer had outgrown them, and as her parents' medical practices had grown and their time for their daughter had become shorter.

"Well, *I* didn't forget," her dad said, sitting down across from her in the breakfast nook. "I just got too busy and let my priorities get out of whack. Will you let me make up for it a little?"

"Sure," Jennifer said and smiled. "But, let me see . . . do I get a little extra allowance for all this free shopping time I'm going to have?"

The phone rang.

"Saved by the bell," her dad said, laughing, as he picked up the receiver. "For you," he said, holding it out to her.

It was Leah, who gave Jennifer a capsule version of everything that had happened.

"Wow, you really miss a lot when you work the night shift," Jennifer said. "I mean this is all just too bizarre. Does Caitlin know?"

"We don't know," Leah said. "Patti might've told her."

"I'll call her and if she *doesn't* already know, I'll break the news gently. You call Patti and the three of you get over here as soon as you can. We need to come up with something, *and fast!*"

"Are you going to let me in on all this?" Jennifer's father asked when she'd hung up.

Jennifer did her best to explain the sequence of events that had occurred since yesterday afternoon.

"But why would Brice rob a convenience store?" Dr. Novak asked. "His father could buy him a dozen of them."

"Brice is a weird guy," Jennifer said. "You can't ask reasonable questions about his behavior. Apparently he's interested in Caitlin and thinks Dom is the only obstacle in his way. So he found a way to put him out of commission."

Her father shook his head. "Boy! And I thought all the excitement was at the hospital. I ought to stay home more mornings."

"Believe me," she said, giving him a sleepy hug.

"They're not all as mondo bizarro as this."

Caitlin and Patti were the first to show up at Jennifer's. Caitlin was distraught. Usually, she was pin neat. This morning, though, she looked as though she'd come over straight out of bed, which Jennifer then realized she probably had. Jennifer put her arms around her friend and gave her a hug.

"We're going to fix this, don't worry," she told Caitlin, although she didn't really have the faintest idea how they were going to do this.

Dr. Novak put on a new pot of coffee and started making fried eggs for everyone. Jennifer winced, but there was no stopping him.

"I'll be like the White House chef," he said. "While the big decisions are being made, I'll be at the stove, feeding the decision makers."

Jennifer smiled. It was the first time in a long while that her dad had been around for her like this. She could tell he realized this, too, and was trying to make up for lost time.

Caitlin was not getting better. She had started crying.

"Why didn't you tell me?" she asked Patti, who apparently had been down at the police station most of the night while her father tried, unsuccessfully, to come up with bail for Dom, which had been set at $10,000.

"I knew you'd be upset. At first we thought it was some big mistake, and everything would be cleared up by this morning."

"It *was* a mistake," Caitlin practically screamed.

"*We* know that," Patti said. "Convincing the police is another story. Everyone saw a black pickup like his in the 7-Eleven parking lot. His keys were found on the pavement. *And*, he has no alibi. He says he was alone at the time of the crime. Out taking a walk, he said."

"Just when *did* the robbery occur?" Caitlin asked.

"About one-thirty yesterday afternoon."

"He was with me," Caitlin said, her voice now barely a whisper. "I picked him up at home. It was his day off. We went out to the canoe camp. It's kind of our private place. He's covering for me. I can vouch for him."

"Yeah, right," Jennifer said sarcastically. "They're really going to be impressed with his girl-friend's word on the matter."

Leah and Danny came through the kitchen door. They'd gone back one more time to try to persuade Sergeant Becker that Brice was the one he should have in custody.

"You think Brice did it?" Jennifer's dad asked Danny.

"Leah's our eyewitness. She was there on the floor all through the holdup," Danny said.

"I saw his shoes," Leah said. "And nobody else wears shoes like that. It was Brice all right. And it's my guess he's also the one who's been lifting all that cash out of the men's lockers at the club. He wants to put Dom out of the running so he can have a clear path to the heart of our darling little Caitlin."

Caitlin blushed and gave Leah a playful shove. Then Caitlin got serious again. "But how did he get hold of Dom's truck?" she wondered aloud.

"Oh, it would've been easy enough," Patti said. "Nobody was at our house yesterday. My mom had the little ones at the day care center, and I was at work, and Dom was with you."

"But how did he get the keys?"

"Same way he got all those wallets," Danny said. "Took them out of Dom's locker, made dupes, went and got the truck, drove over to the 7-Eleven, dropped Dom's set on the ground for a bit of incriminating evidence, then used the dupes to drive the truck back to the Costas'. Left the truck and went back to the club. Or home. Brice is weird, but he's also pretty smart."

"What're you kids going to do, though?" Dr. Novak asked. "I mean, you've got me believing Brice is the culprit, but how are you going to convince the police?"

Everyone sat silent for a moment, thinking.

"What if," Jennifer said in the middle of buttering a piece of toast, "what if we set a trap for him."

"Like a giant net?" Leah said.

"Sort of," Jennifer said, and they all began offering suggestions, putting in their ideas on a collaboration they wound up calling "OGB: Operation Get Brice."

Chapter 20

The day was mild, the first break in the relentless heat of the past few weeks, so Caitlin could ride her horse hard across the plains and then into the small woods at the edge of Hickory Hills. When she reached a clearing by a small stream — one of many mountain streams that fed into the Rio Rojo — she dismounted and led Honky Tonk, a copper mare with jet black mane and tail, over to the softly rushing water. Then she sat down, pulled her boots off, and put her feet into the icy water, touching the cool stones along its bottom with her toes.

This was her most private place. She hadn't even brought Dom here. (Yet, anyway.) Whenever she needed to be alone to think, this is where she came. And today, she *really* needed to think. Dom was in jail because of her, because he didn't want to say he'd been with her the whole time the holdup was going on.

The rain dancers would get him out of jail. Jennifer's father and Danny's dad were at the bank now, coming up with enough to make bail. But unless the rain dancers' plan to trap Brice worked — and she wasn't sure it would — Dom would still be the chief suspect in the case. She was the only one who could provide him with an alibi. But to do that would mean admitting to the police — and to her parents — that she had been seeing Dom all along, even though they had forbidden her to.

Plus her father's anger might not stop at her and Dom. He might take it out on Mr. Costa, who was supposed to have been making sure his son kept away from Caitlin. She knew her father's temper well enough to know he was capable of firing Dom's dad over this.

She sat dangling her feet in the stream for half an hour or so, but remained stuck at the same impasse in her mind. If she came forward and admitted she and Dom had been together yesterday afternoon out at the canoe camp (when she'd told her mother she was going to the library), she might save Dom, but at the same time hurt his family. The Costas were already struggling financially and could hardly afford a father out of work. But if she kept quiet about having been with Dom, he might actually go to prison for a crime he didn't commit.

She was trapped between truth and deception, between lesser evil and greater good. And the conclusion she finally came to was that she needed to talk with Dom. This was a decision they needed to make *together*.

When she got back to the house, she came in the side door and took the back stairs up to her room, hoping to avoid her mother. Once inside, she shut the door, flopped onto her water bed, and grabbed the phone off the floor so she could call the Novak house.

"It's all done," Jennifer told her when she picked up at her end. "My dad and Danny's put up the bail. They'll be letting Dom out within the next couple of hours. Patti and I are going down there to get him."

"No," Caitlin said. "I'll go. I want to be there for him. I want him to see that I'm there."

She didn't even bother changing out of her old riding jeans and dusty boots; she just grabbed her keys and ran out to the garage to get her Miata and kicked up gravel all the way down the drive.

She'd been driving almost an hour in the parking lot behind the police station when he came out the door. Her heart soared. She tried not to let this show completely. She was a little embarrassed at having this much feeling for him, let alone showing it.

"I was just driving by the jail and thought I'd stop by and see if there were any cute prisoners I might like to pick up and take home," she said as he stood outside of the car, looking down at her.

"Then you really should wait a little longer. The guy I shared the cell with should have slept off his drunken spree anytime now. I think he might be your type."

"No," she said. "I think *you* are definitely my type. Hop in."

He jumped into the passenger seat. "I can't believe Danny and Jennifer's fathers pitched in to get me out."

"Yeah. They're good guys. You see, *all* of the rain dancers' parents aren't such terrible snobs as mine." She felt tears welling up in her eyes, then the pressure of Dom's thumb brushing lightly across her closed eyelid.

"Oh, Caitlin," he said, wrapping his arms around her, burying his face in her hair.

"Dom, it was so awful knowing you were in there."

"Confirmed all your parents' worst suspicions, I'll bet," he said.

"I haven't had to face them yet. You made the front page of this morning's paper, but I ducked my mom, and my dad never reads the news until he gets to work. I can just see him gloating at his desk, though."

"I didn't tell them," he said, nodding toward the police station to indicate he meant the police. "You know. About you and me."

Caitlin put her forehead against his and said, "I didn't either." She explained the tug of war going on inside her, then told him about the plan the rain dancers had come up with to catch Brice.

"Well," Dom said, "if it works, they'll have the real thief, and I won't need an alibi." He looked around at the beautiful day. "You can't know how great it is to be outside after a night in *there*."

"I've been frantic since I found out," Caitlin said. "I knew I loved you before, but it wasn't until you were locked away from me that I saw how impossible it would be not to have you in my life now that I've been as happy as I have this summer."

"Oh, Cait," he said, as he grabbed a handful of hair at the back of her head and leaned across to kiss her with an intensity she had never before experienced.

Jennifer and her dad came back from Dallas Sunday night. She went straight over to Alan's house. She'd had a great time, too great probably. She felt guilty having so much fun when Alan couldn't.

His mother answered the door. "Oh, Jen, it's good to see you," she said, leading Jennifer back into the den. "Try to cheer him up a bit, will you? He's been having a bad day."

The den smelled disturbingly like a room at the hospital — stuffy, the air used up by the sickness. She was taken aback when she first saw him. Being away for a couple of days let her see his decline in a way she hadn't until now. Not that anything major had changed since Friday. He was still weak and depressed. Also, lately, he had begun to tune in and out of conversations, as though his attention was a weak station at the far end of the radio dial.

"Where've you been?" he said, lifting himself slowly up off the couch in the den where he was lying, watching TV.

"Honey," she said. "I told you. My dad took me to Dallas with him."

"Dallas," Alan said and sank back down onto the stack of pillows he was propped on. Jennifer still wasn't sure he understood. She also couldn't help noticing that the orientation packet from UCLA was still lying, unopened, on the coffee table next to him, by now marked with the rings of a hundred cans of soda and cups of tea. "Did you have a good time?" he asked.

"Yeah," she said, feeling almost as though she was confessing something. "We went to some cool restaurants. I went to three art museums and bought an incredible leather jacket. I figured I need to have something ultracool to make my impression on Hollywood." She felt almost traitorous even mentioning going to L.A. But why? She wasn't sure. "The whole weekend was cool, really," she went on. "Plus it was good spending time with my dad. He seems to have realized he's been shortchanging me and Scotty. He seems hellbent on making up for lost time. He's taking Scotty down to see the Alamo next month, just before the monster has to go back to school. It's kind of weird with him paying us all this attention after years of pretty much ignoring us, but . . ."

She stopped here. She realized that although Alan's eyes were open, he wasn't really seeing her or hearing what she was saying.

"What are you thinking about?" she asked him, getting up and coming over to sit on the edge of the sofa next to him. She pressed her cheek to his chest. She could feel his breastbone under its now thin covering of skin. She could feel the shallowness of his breaths as his chest rose and fell slightly. She looked up into his face and waited for his answer, but none came. Tears came running out of the corners of his eyes, onto his cheeks as he shook his head from side to side, as if to say "no."

"Come on," she said. "You can tell me, no matter what it is."

He smiled a rueful smile and said, "I was thinking of those dumb essays teachers always used to make us write in grade school when we came back in the fall. You know. 'How I Spent My Summer Vacation.' Mine would have to be, 'I Spent My Summer Dying.'"

Chapter 21

On Wednesday, "Operation Get Brice" went into action. The rain dancers had lain low for a few days, figuring Brice would be behaving for a while following his big event at the 7-Eleven.

Caitlin played the first part in the scheme.

"Hey, Brice," she said, passing "accidentally" by the caddy shack first thing in the morning, when she knew he wouldn't be out on the course yet. He was a fairly awful caddy and was usually one of the last chosen by members. "How's it going?" she said, stopping to lean against the porch railing of the shack.

"Oh, not too bad," Brice said. At first he looked a little surprised that she was paying him this attention, but then his massive ego kicked in and he recovered quickly. "Haven't seen too much of you this summer," he went on. "I gather you've been '*occupado*.' " He underlined the word as he said it.

"Yeah, but that was before I found out he was a major criminal. I guess there's something to my parents' advice. You know — stick to your own social class."

"That's always been *my* policy," Brice said smugly, as though the two of them were finally on the same wavelength.

"I think — poor boy — he must've done it to get enough money to take me out in style. You know, I like to go to Le Figaro and Playa del Sol, places like that. They were a little beyond his means, I'm afraid."

"He was just running in company that was a little too fast for him," Brice said.

"I've heard some people think he might be behind all those thefts around here. That would just be too much. I mean I guess you could forgive someone for robbing an impersonal store, but robbing people — people I *know*! I just never could forgive that."

"Say," Brice said, seeing his opening, "as long as you're down on him, how about going out for an elegant dinner with me this weekend? Say, at Luxe?" Luxe was the most expensive restaurant in River Bend.

"Why, Brice, that sounds like a nice idea, a *very* nice idea."

Three minutes later, Caitlin was scuttling around the clubhouse, into the pool area. She collapsed in a gale of laughter against the wall where Jennifer and Patti were waiting for her.

"I gather it went well?" Patti asked.

"Like a charm," Caitlin said. "Now it's Dom's turn."

Dom drove the utility truck past the caddy shack and pulled over beneath a large tree across from it.

"Hey, Costa," Brice called out. "Hear you got caught with your hand in the cookie jar."

Dom ignored this, got out his pruning shears, and stood in the back of the truck.

"I guess you were trying to impress your girl-friend — or should I say *ex*-girlfriend?" Brice taunted. "If you want my advice, I say stay with your own kind. Find yourself a nice, ordinary girl, marry her, and have a houseful of ordinary babies. Like your parents did."

It took everything in Dom to resist jumping down off the truckbed and throttling Brice. But he had to stick to his part in the operation. Which was to reach up high enough so that the handkerchief barely stuffed into his back pocket fell to the ground. It was an old linen monogrammed handkerchief, with "DC" embroidered in the corner. Dom had a drawer full of these, a legacy from his grandfather, who had also been Dominick Costa.

When Dom had "accidentally" dropped the hand-kerchief and cut the branch and driven off, Leah watched through the window of the pro shop. She was pretending to be interested in buying some ten-nis balls, but was actually checking to make sure Phase Two of the operation was going according to plan. She smiled when she saw Brice go over and pick the handkerchief up off the ground. She could almost see him put two and two together and come up with five.

"All *right*!" she said under her breath. It was time for Dr. Novak and Mr. Sanchez to play golf.

"I just need a Class-B caddy today, Doug," Dr. Novak said to Doug Fletcher, the club's caddymaster.

"I can give you Hector Gonzales," Jim said.

"Uh, what about Brice Fraser?" Dr. Novak said. "I thought I saw him around. I had him the other day."

"You had him before and you want him *again*?" Jim asked with disbelief. "We don't usually get second requests for Brice."

"Well, his father's a friend of mine and, well, you know . . ."

"Say no more, Dr. Novak. I'll have him get your clubs."

Dr. Novak and Danny's father only played nine holes before they headed back to shower and change. Nine holes gave them plenty of opportunity to mention the high stakes they were playing for in a complicated betting system called "Nassau."

"You're going to owe me several hundred dollars by the time we're through," Mr. Sanchez baited Dr. Novak. "Did you remember to bring your checkbook? Because I take Visa at my restaurant, but not for gambling debts."

"Better than that," Dr. Novak said, patting his back pocket which showed the outline of a fat wallet inside. "I'm prepared to pay in cold cash. That is, *if* you win."

Which they made sure Mr. Sanchez did. And when they were done and in the locker room, they made sure to ostentatiously transfer the winnings — $700 — from Dr. Novak's wallet to Mr. Sanchez's. The wallet then hung in his pants pocket while both of the men went off to shower.

It only took Brice about two minutes to find his way into Danny's father's locker and get his hands on the wallet.

And it only took Ken Tyler — who had been tipped off — two seconds to step out from around the end of the row of lockers as Brice was taking the cash out of the wallet and planting his "incriminating evidence," Dom's handkerchief, in front of the open locker.

"Brice, I believe your days at this club are over," Ken said.

The rain dancers, standing outside when Mr. Tyler came out with a vise grip on Brice's elbow, burst into applause.

Brice glared at them as he passed by, realizing the trap he'd fallen into. His face turned so red with rage, it almost got purple.

"What happened then?" Alan asked Jennifer later when she'd stopped by to fill him in on their evil plot. He was having one of his better days and was curious about what was happening in the world without him.

"Well, it wasn't easy, considering who Brice's father is, but with some pressure from my dad and Danny's, the police issued a search warrant and went out to the compound and into Brice's room. Where I'm sure you'll be astonished to hear they found a hollowed-out book on the shelf filled with cash — the two thousand from the 7-Eleven holdup and most of what he'd taken from the members' lockers."

"But they weren't *marked bills* like in the movies," Alan said.

"Too bad, eh?" Jennifer said. "Much more nicely incriminating was the duplicate set of Dom's truck keys Brice had been too stupid or arrogant to get rid of."

"You've almost got me feeling sorry for the poor guy."

Jennifer stared him down.

"Well, I said *almost*."

"So Dom is cleared of all charges — much to the disappointment of Mr. and Mrs. Carney I don't suppose I have to add — and Brice will probably be off to something a little stricter than an Ivy League college. A place with a lot of *structure*, if you get my drift."

Alan started laughing at Jennifer's gleeful telling of the story.

"You're just so proud of your little scheme, aren't you?" he said, tickling her.

"Well, I guess I am," she said, trying to dodge his tickling fingers. They roughhoused on the sofa like this until Alan broke out in spasms of coughing.

Jennifer went and got him some water and sat back down next to him. "I'd trap a crook every day if I could get you to laugh like that," she said.

Alan said thoughtfully, "I know what you mean. Most of all, I miss laughing with you."

September

Chapter 22

The trees at the canoe camp were beginning to turn. Their rustling now had a dry sound, the sound of autumn approaching. These were the last stolen days of summer and both Dom and Caitlin knew it. They had been avoiding the subject of fall and what it would mean to them, to their relationship. But the change in seasons was a sign. It was going to be impossible to ignore these questions much longer.

Still, they tried to live in the moment, even though these might be their last ones. Today, of course, they were filled with wanting to talk about Brice, about the holdup, his plots, his twisted personality. He had confessed, not only to the thefts at the club, but also to the 7-Eleven robbery. One of Dom's old buddies, who was now a cop in River Bend, told him Brice's confession was more like bragging, as though he wanted to take credit for the crimes. Now he was out on bail, waiting for his trial date. It didn't look like his father's money would be of any help to him now.

"But *why* was Brice stealing from the members, do you think?" Dom asked her as they were lying side by side on the dock.

"I guess he likes to think of himself as above everyone else. Working at the club this summer put him *below* a lot of people. The stealing was probably just a way to even things up."

"And that's why he wanted to get me, too?"

"No, I think he wanted to get to *me* and thought you were the big obstacle in his way."

"I can just see you and old Bricebrain together," Dom said. "Of course, your parents would be thrilled. It would be like one of those marriages between one land-owning family and another. Then all of River Bend would belong to you. I'd just be some guy back in the servants' quarters."

"Where I'd be sneaking off to every night," Caitlin said. She rolled over onto her stomach and looked between the warped and weathered slats of the mooring dock, down into the water below. She looked over at Dom, who had his eyes closed.

"You're looking at me," he said. "I can feel it."

"Okay, if you're so perceptive, why don't you also tell me what I'm thinking," she teased him.

"I can probably guess," he said.

She traced a finger lightly across his dark eyebrows. "Oh, Dom, what are we going to do?"

"I think it's really more a question of what *you're* going to do," he said.

And once again, there they were, back at Square One. This time, though, she wasn't going to let all the responsibility fall to her.

"Why?" she said.

"Why what?" he said.

"Why is the issue what *I'm* going to do?" she asked.

"Well, you're the one who's either staying here with me or going off to college."

"But couldn't we put it another way?" she said, sitting up. Suddenly she didn't feel like being so close to him. She didn't want to be physically vulnerable while she was tying to make her point. She didn't want him to throw her off balance with a kiss. "Couldn't we say the question was whether you're going to come away with me or stay here in River Bend?"

"Go along with you to *college*?!" he said.

"I still haven't made up my mind if I'm going to college in the fall, but I do know I want to see something of the rest of the world before I decide whether or not I'm going to settle down here."

"But I've already seen the world," he protested.

"How nice for you."

"Well, I can tell you that, when you've seen the rest of it, River Bend looks pretty good," he said.

"To *you*," Caitlin pointed out, feeling the fire glowing behind her eyes. "You've had the experience *for* me, then. So I don't have to have it myself. Give me a break."

He didn't say anything. She could feel him

tensing. He wasn't used to her contradicting him.

"Look," she said. "If I stay here on account of you, I'll only wind up resenting you for asking me to do it. I was born here. I've lived here for eighteen years. Who knows, maybe I'll die here. But right now I need to be away from here, getting my head turned around, seeing how life is lived in other places. You needed to do the same thing, so don't deny it to me."

"But this is different," he said. "You're a girl."

"No," Caitlin said, standing up. "According to my welcome packet from Vassar, I'm now a woman."

"Hey, where are you going?" he asked nervously, jumping up and following her off the dock.

"Back to town," she said, walking over to the Miata. Seeing it parked next to Dom's huge, ancient black pickup just underlined the differences between them. What had at first seemed like interesting contrasts now seemed like unbridgeable chasms.

She jumped into her car, gunned the motor, and raised a cloud of dust around Dom as she peeled out toward the highway.

She felt both horribly sad and at the same time exhilarated. She was disappointing the most important people in her life, but she was also — for the first time — asking herself what *she* wanted, which felt like a big step toward finding out who Caitlin Carney really was.

And while she was figuring herself out, she was

also going to do her best to help a friend who needed a chance to find out who *she* was.

Between three-forty-five and four that afternoon, all the rain dancers' paths crossed, without any of them being aware of it.

Danny came out of Ed's Barber Shop on Arkansas Street just as Caitlin's blue car turned the corner onto Lone Star Avenue.

Caitlin, on her way home, had just turned right from Lone Star onto San Antonio Way when Jennifer, on her bike, turned left onto Lone Star *from* San Antonio Way.

A few minutes later, Jennifer, on her way to Alan's house, passed right by Leah, who was in a phone booth further south on Lone Star, in front of the Chinese carryout shop, calling Danny, leaving a message on his tape about the meeting of the rain dancers that Caitlin had called her about this morning.

The only one left out of this loop was Patti.

Danny walked into his house, found Leah's message, and called her back. "So everything's set for tonight?" he asked.

"Yeah. Caitlin said why didn't we just meet at the grill. At eight. It's Patti's night off, so she won't be around. Actually, given how much she loves her job, the grill's the one place we can be sure she *won't* turn up."

"What's wrong?" Dom asked his sister, coming into the Costas' living room, where she was lying on the sofa with the telephone resting on her stomach.

She looked up at him sharply, as though she'd been a million miles away.

"Huh? Oh. Well, nothing," she said.

"Glad I asked," Dom teased, crumpling into the recliner across from the sofa.

"Oh, Dom, I don't know. All summer, I've been feeling more and more excluded from the old group. Shut out. Like I know Caitlin and Jennifer and Leah all went to Echo Mall last weekend to shop for clothes for college. And they didn't ask me along."

"But you're not going to college, so they knew you wouldn't need any college clothes."

"I know. That's just it. That's what's separating me from them. They're all going off to exciting lives while I'm staying here. They've already started to forget me. Like tonight's my night off, and I've tried calling all the rain dancers. Danny's sister said he went to "a meeting." What kind of meeting would he be going to? I mean he doesn't belong to anything. Leah's phone doesn't answer; I've tried twice. Jennifer's mother has no idea where Jen is — of course. I mean when does Jen's mother *ever* know where Jen is? And Caitlin's tape says to leave a message, but I didn't bother."

"I know," Dom said. "I tried calling her myself.

"Hey. Why don't you and I go to the movies?"

"Are you serious? I thought you wouldn't be caught dead out in public with your kid sister."

"That was when I was an immature high school boy. Now I'm a sophisticated man of the world. Mr.

Sophistication. So of course I'd be happy to be seen with my terrific sister."

"Oh, Dom. That's so sweet."

"Just one thing," he said, pushing the recliner back to its upright position.

"Yeah?"

"Would you mind walking a few steps behind me and wearing a paper bag over your head?"

He didn't duck fast enough to get out of the way of a barrage of small pillows.

On the way into town in the pickup, Patti asked Dom, "Can we stop by the club for a second? I left my sweatshirt at work, and those theaters out at the mall are air-conditioned like meat lockers."

"No problem," he said and turned the volume up on the radio. One thing that hadn't changed with Mr. Sophistication was that he liked his rock and roll loud.

When they pulled up at the back entrance to the grill, Dom left the engine running and the radio on while Patti hopped down out of the cab and up to the kitchen before she noticed that, even though this was the night the grill was closed, all the lights were on. She had her hand on the door knob before she looked through the window and saw a scene that broke her heart — the other rain dancers all gathered, clearly in the middle of some lively plans about something.

And she'd been excluded.

Chapter 23

Patti sat up in her room. It was really the attic of her family's home, but she had fixed it up, and at least it gave her some privacy. Which she desperately needed at the moment.

She hadn't told Dom what she'd seen through the window at the grill. He was absorbed in his music and his thoughts and when she got back in the cab of his truck, she told him she'd forgotten that she'd left her sweatshirt at Caitlin's, not at the club and she'd be okay without it. He bought the story and put the truck in gear.

She barely saw the movie. The scene that was playing and replaying in her mind was the one she'd seen through the grill's kitchen window. The scene of all her friends discussing something. They'd been talking among themselves so excitedly. But about what? And were old Mr. Oakley and Doc McPherson and Caitlin's father really there, too? Or had she only imagined them in the scene? Why would the three richest men in town be meeting with the rain dancers? Or, at least, four-fifths of the rain dancers.

Up in her room, at least she — the fifth rain dancer — didn't have to hold back the tears.

Caitlin found Dom out on the sixth-hole fairway, raking up and bagging the first of the fall leaves. She looked at him in his worn jeans and high-top sneakers, his muscled arms straining against the red T-shirt he was wearing, and felt the coldness she'd been trying to maintain toward him begin to melt.

She came up to him slowly, crushing the leaves beneath her feet. He looked up and saw her, but didn't stop to say hello.

"Aren't you speaking to me?" she asked.

He stopped and leaned against the rake. "*You're the one who left in a big snit the other day*," he said.

She walked up and put her arms around him. "Let's stop, all right? Stop being stupid with each other. I've only got a few days left here, and I don't want us to spend them fighting." She felt his arms wrapping around her.

"I know," he said softly, his mouth pressed against her ear. (It always amazed her that someone who looked so rough could be so gentle.) "I'm going to be without you soon enough — when you go to college. I don't want to be without you any sooner than I have to. These past few days have torn me up."

Caitlin pulled back from him and walked over to a giant old oak tree and tugged free a small cluster of leaves. "I'm not going to college," she told him.

"You're not?!" Dom said, and she could see his face light up with happiness, which made her feel terrible as she rushed to finish what she had to tell him. "I want to go to Paris."

"Paris?" He looked completely bewildered.

"I told you I need to see something of the world. Something beyond River Bend," she said. "Paris has been a dream place in my mind for a long time."

"But, how . . . ?"

"I've gotten an application for a language program there for foreigners. The students live in apartments. There are cultural field trips. It sounds really great."

"But how are you going to pay for it?"

"My grandfather left me a trust fund. Now that I'm eighteen, I can use the money any way I want. Not even my parents can stop me."

"You've told them?"

Caitlin nodded. "At first my dad went ballistic. He really hates when my mom or I do something without getting his approval first. But when he had a little time to think about it and talk with my mother . . . well, you know they're terrible snobs. I guess being able to say their daughter is in Paris has as much status value as saying I'm at Vassar."

"Paris," Dom said, shaking his head. "You must've wanted to get as far away from me as possible."

"Dom, come with me. That's what I want you to do. Think of the fun we'd have."

This stopped him in his tracks. "But how could I afford that?"

"You wouldn't have to. My trust fund is *not* a small one."

He shook his head. "I just couldn't do that. Let you support me."

"Well, it would really be letting my grandfather support us both."

"No! I just couldn't. I make my own way in the world."

They stood looking at each other and, for a long moment suspended in time, they were without the words necessary to say all the things they were thinking, wishing. Then Dom dropped the rake to the ground and came over to where she was standing and put his hands on either side of her head, his hands flat against the rough bark as he kissed her with a mixture of tenderness and passion that astonished her.

"Please," she whispered in his ear, "come away with me."

"Please," he whispered back, "stay here with me."

She pushed him away far enough that she could look him hard in the eyes.

"I love you," she told him, "but I can't stay here."

He nodded and dropped his arms to his sides.

"Now you're mad again," she guessed, but he shook his head.

"No. Just incredibly sad," he said and walked over and picked up the fallen rake. Then he tossed the bags full of leaves into the back of the greenskeeper cart and hopped into the driver's seat. He didn't look back as he drove off down the fairway, over a hill, and out of sight.

Caitlin stood there by the oak tree thinking, *Why does love have to be so complicated?*

Danny came down between the rows of bookshelves until he got to the end where Leah was reshelving a cart full of books.

"Hi!" he whispered.

"Hi," she said, then giggled at how quiet he was trying to be.

"I could never work here," he said in a low voice. "My shoes squeak too much."

"We librarians use a professional product — Squeak-Away."

He almost believed this until he saw the glint of mischief in her eye. He reached over and gave her a fake pinch.

"Can you get out of here for a while?" he asked. He was leaving for Vermont early the next morning, and his family was throwing him a big farewell party tonight, so this would be the last time he could talk with Leah alone.

She knew this and nodded. "I'll just have to ask the boss. She's usually a soft touch, though."

They sat on the front steps of the library. For a while, neither of them said anything. They just sat and watched people walking or driving by. River Bend was a small enough town that they knew almost everyone who went past.

"It's going to be weird going someplace where I

don't already know everyone," he said. "And where it's going to be so, I don't know — Vermonty."

"Hills and snow," Leah said.

"Right. How do you think Tex-Mex cooking will go over in Vermont?"

"You mean enchiladas with maple syrup? I don't know. Could be a culinary breakthrough. I'm nervous about going away, and I'm only going to Austin. Still, I'm going to have to make all new friends, and I'm totally out of practice. I haven't made a new friend in years."

"But you're not going to forget your old ones, are you?" Danny said, looking down at the concrete steps as though they were fascinating, afraid to meet her eyes as he asked the question.

Leah smiled and put two fingers under his chin and turned his face toward her. "No way. How could I? The rain dancers are practically family to me."

He was pretty sure she was just teasing him, but he had to make sure. "Does that mean you think of me as a brother?"

She answered by kissing him long and slow. When they had pulled back out of the kiss, he looked around nervously, and Leah laughed.

"Don't worry. Librarians have special privileges. We're allowed to kiss anyone we want on library property. Don't try this with any other girls, though, or you'll probably get arrested."

"I wouldn't think of kissing any other girls."

"Not even cute Vermont girls who yodel?"

This cracked him up. He had to stop laughing before he could say, "I think that's Switzerland you're thinking of. I think Vermont is mountains, but without the yodeling or the cuckoo clocks."

"Can I visit you there?"

"You bet!" Danny said. "Why don't we plan for you to come out for Thanksgiving? I can pay for your ticket. We'll have four days to . . ."

"Yes . . . ?" she said, forcing him to come up with an end to his sentence.

"To explore the state's natural splendors and engage in wholesome outdoor athletic activities."

"You mean no kissing all weekend?"

"Well, maybe a couple at the airport when we say good-bye," he teased her back.

"You know," she said, putting her hand on his, "this time we've had together has been really nice."

Someone roared by on a motorcycle. Danny saw a mild look of annoyance cross Leah's face while she waited for the noise to go away so she could finish what she was saying to him.

"I feel like I've been getting to know a whole side of you I never saw when we were just friends."

"You've found out that by night I'm a *vam*pire!" he said, giving her neck a fake bite.

"Well, that, of course. But really, I used to just think you were manic . . ."

"And now you know I'm depressive, too," Danny said. He always felt more comfortable goofing than being serious. But Leah wasn't going to let him slide away with jokes this time.

"I've found out that underneath your joke-a-minute exterior, you're really very sensitive and sweet."

"Awwww," he said. "I'm blushing."

"No, you're not. Because you know it's the truth. And it's your sensitive side that's made me care about you in this new way."

"By 'new way,' do you mean a love kind of way?"

"I'm not sure. Actually, I'm not sure I even know what love is, yet. Maybe I need to grow into the emotion."

"So where does that leave us?"

"Well," Leah said. "In process? It's really not all that long until Thanksgiving break. And in the meantime, there are — I hear — such things as long distance phone calls and those little pieces of paper you put into envelopes . . ."

"Letters!" Danny said, laughing.

"That's it," Leah said. "So, what do you say we keep on seeing what's happening between us."

"Deal," Danny said, putting out his hand to shake on it. But Leah used the hand to pull him toward her for a kiss.

"No respect for public places," Mrs. Tesch, one of the town's most curmudgeonly old women, said to her husband as they walked past Danny and Leah on their way up the steps to the library.

"My mother will kill me if they tell her they saw us," Leah said, but she was laughing so hard Danny knew she wasn't really scared. He knew, too, that things between them really did stand a chance. Sure they'd be in different states, but so what? Wasn't there a saying, "Absence makes the heart grow fonder"? And now there was one thing he knew he no longer had to worry about. That motorcycle that had roared by, the one Leah had only looked at as a noise pollutant — it had been Greg Wright's.

Jennifer was up in Caitlin's bedroom, lying on her friend's water bed, watching her pack.

"Boy, Paris," Jennifer said. "I still can't quite believe it. Neither can the others."

"I know," Caitlin said. "If you want to know the truth, I'm kind of scared, going so far away and all. But in another way, it just feels great, like I'm being released into the air and can finally fly."

"You and Danny are taking the same bus tomorrow morning?"

Caitlin nodded. "Yeah. We go to Houston, then catch a bus to the airport and fly to New York together. So I'll have company on at least the first part of the trip. Are you going to see us off?"

"Sure. I'll just come straight over from the hospital."

"When do you leave — Thursday is it?"

"Well," Jennifer said. "The thing is, I've had a slight change of plans, myself."

Caitlin stopped in the middle of folding a sweater. "Like?"

"Like I'm not going."

"Not going? Not going to UCLA on a full scholarship? Not following the one dream you have? Why not?"

"Alan. My dad doesn't think he has that much time left. If that's true, I want to be with him for however long it is."

"But won't you lose the scholarship?"

"Yes, but I'm not telling him that," Jennifer said, "so don't mention it. He's already going to have enough problems with me staying without adding that to his burden of guilt."

"Oh, Jen, I can see how you want to stay with him, but . . ." she trailed off there.

"See?" Jennifer said. "You can't really come up with a justification for my leaving. I mean, how could I do it? How could I go to classes every day and be meeting all sorts of exciting people and live with the knowledge that Alan was back here, lying on that couch in his den, watching *Family Feud* — alone?"

"This is just so awful for you," Caitlin said.

"Not as awful as it is for Alan," Jennifer said as Caitlin sat down on the water bed and hugged her.

As they rocked back and forth a little, Caitlin said, "What a summer this has been."

"Phone for Patti!" Mr. Costa shouted up the stairs.

She ran down the attic steps and picked up the phone in the upstairs hall. It was Caitlin.

"You busy tonight?" she asked.

"You know, it's funny," Patti said, "but I'm not. Tyler just called and said there'd been a mix-up in the schedule and I'm really supposed to be off tonight. Why?" She was wary of her friends, including Caitlin, since seeing them all together without her.

"Oh, I just thought you and I might grab a bite at Pizza Joe's. Maybe go to the show later."

"But isn't this your last night here? Don't you

want to be spending it with someone . . . well someone special?"

"If you are referring to your brother, he's too angry with me for leaving to want to celebrate my last night in town, I'm afraid."

"I wondered what was going on with you two. He's just shut up like a clam. Well, what about your parents?"

"Tonight's their couple counseling therapist night. They can't miss a session. It might be fatal, if you know what I mean."

Patti laughed. "Well, I guess some things never change."

"Listen, Patti. It sounds to me like you're trying to get out of seeing me tonight. I can take a hint."

"No, no. I'd love to go for pizza."

"Great. I'll pick you up at seven."

"But this isn't the way into town," Patti said when Caitlin sped away from the Costa house, out onto the plains, which were an eerie flat gray at night, lit only by moonlight.

"I'm kidnapping you," Caitlin said.

"If the ransom's more than two ninety-five, my parents won't be able to pay it."

Caitlin just kept driving. "No further information will be given to the kidnapee."

"Caitlin!"

But Caitlin just shook her head and kept on driving into the night. They went several miles until finally Caitlin turned off the highway at the entrance to the old canoe camp. When they came to the end of the dirt drive and came out into the clearing of trees by the river, Patti saw a big campfire with three silhouetted figures standing around it. When they got closer and Caitlin stopped the car, Patti could see the figures were Leah and Jennifer and Danny. They were all wearing Apache headdresses, looking much as they had that day of the first rain dance, so many years ago.

"Hey, what is this?" she said, getting out of the car.

Caitlin handed her a headband with feathers flowing out from it. "Put it on."

"What for?"

"We're dancing to see if we can make it rain for you."

"For me?"

"Yes. Now come and sit in our pow wow circle," she said, pointing to a place on the ground around the fire, where the other rain dancers were now sitting in a loose circle.

"All right, all right," Patti said, still without a clue as to what was going on.

"Chief Leah will announce the good news," Danny said.

"Thank you brave warrior Daniel," Leah said. "We are here tonight to bestow on our fellow rain dancer, Patricia, something she mightily deserves — "

"Huh?" Patti said, still trying to adjust her headband.

"A full scholarship to the University of Texas in the city of Austin in our great Lone Star State."

"What? Are you guys kidding around?"

"Nope," Danny said. "We are really for real. You and Leah are riding up there together next week."

"But what about my job?"

"Regrettably," Danny said. "I've had to fire you. You were overqualified, I'm afraid. You carried that tray too efficiently. You were ruining everyone else's morale. So you see, I had to let you go."

"But how did you come up with the money — robbing the 7-Eleven?"

Jennifer shook her head. "No, for some reason, they were out of cash. So we had a talk with certain well-heeled members at the club, and we persuaded them that you would be the absolutely most suitable recipient of the annual Employees Scholarship."

"Employees Scholarship? I didn't even know there was such a thing," Patti said, still amazed. "I mean, wow."

"There wasn't until we had our persuasive dialogue with Doc McPherson and Will Oakley and my dad," Caitlin said. "And they agreed that a scholarship like that would be a good community act for the club and that you were the perfect person to get the first one."

"Wow," Patti said. "I mean *wow!*"

"Maybe she isn't the right one for this," Jennifer teased. "I mean it does seem her vocabulary is a bit limited."

"Wow," Patti said again. She laughed as she realized that this was what the scene she'd come upon the other night had been all about. And she felt awful for even thinking for a split second that the rain dancers were anything but the best friends she was ever going to have.

The next morning, Caitlin's parents brought her to the bus station, where Danny was already waiting with his whole family. When he saw how much stuff Caitlin was bringing with her, he asked, "Did you buy the entire plane?"

"Well," she teased. "I thought as long as I had you to help me with it . . ."

Jennifer pulled up in her parents' car with Alan beside her. He'd insisted on getting out of bed to come down for this farewell. Leah and Patti arrived a few minutes later with Dom in his pickup. Caitlin couldn't believe he was here. She'd been awake all night thinking about him, thinking she'd never see him again. She was astonished he was here now, both because he'd been so upset with her for leaving and because her parents were here this morning. He didn't let this stop him, though. He hopped down out of the truck, walked up, and took Caitlin by the hand.

"Excuse me," he said to her slightly astonished parents, "but I have a few things to discuss with Caitlin."

Before they could object, he took her by the arm and walked her around to the front of the bus station.

"Look," he said, staring into her eyes, as if to imprint her memory on his brain. "I love you, and if you need to get away from here for a while, then that's what you need to do. I just hope getting away doesn't mean you won't accept visitors from home, because I looked in my date book and found I seem to have a trip to Paris scheduled for sometime around Christmas. I'll tie a red and green ribbon around myself and be your Christmas present. If you want me . . ."

"Oh, Dom!" she cried, but couldn't say any more.

"No time for talking," he said, silencing her mouth with his own. "Just enough time for one last kiss."

The bus was a little early, which made everyone feel their time for good-byes had been cut short. Danny and Caitlin quickly hugged and got hugged back, then got on the bus, found seats, and waved at the others through the murky green windows. Patti and Leah and Jennifer and Dom and Alan stood silently watching the back of the bus disappear into the distant Texas horizon, then turned and looked at each other, knowing that whatever the future held for them, and no matter how many farewells there would be, they would always remain at the center of each other's lives.

About the Author

Carol Stanley is the author of several young adult books including *High School Reunion*, *Second Best Sister*, *The Latchkey Kids*, and *Twin Switch* and has just written her first book for adults, *Aquamarine*. She lives in Chicago.

point®

Other books you will enjoy, about real kids like you!

☐ MZ43469-1	**Arly** Robert Newton Peck	$2.95
☐ MZ40515-2	**City Light** Harry Mazer	$2.75
☐ MZ44494-8	**Enter Three Witches** Kate Gilmore	$2.95
☐ MZ40943-3	**Fallen Angels** Walter Dean Myers	$3.50
☐ MZ40847-X	**First a Dream** Maureen Daly	$3.25
☐ MZ43020-3	**Handsome as Anything** Merrill Joan Gerber	$2.95
☐ MZ43999-5	**Just a Summer Romance** Ann M. Martin	$2.75
☐ MZ44629-0	**Last Dance** Caroline B. Cooney	$2.95
☐ MZ44628-2	**Life Without Friends** Ellen Emerson White	$2.95
☐ MZ42769-3	**Losing Joe's Place** Gordon Korman	$2.95
☐ MZ43664-3	**A Pack of Lies** Geraldine McCaughrean	$2.95
☐ MZ43419-5	**Pocket Change** Kathryn Jensen	$2.95
☐ MZ43821-2	**A Royal Pain** Ellen Conford	$2.95
☐ MZ44429-8	**A Semester in the Life of a Garbage Bag** Gordon Korman	$2.95
☐ MZ43867-0	**Son of Interflux** Gordon Korman	$2.95
☐ MZ43971-5	**The Stepfather Game** Norah McClintock	$2.95
☐ MZ41513-1	**The Tricksters** Margaret Mahy	$2.95
☐ MZ43638-4	**Up Country** Alden R. Carter	$2.95

Watch for new titles coming soon!
Available wherever you buy books, or use this order form.